RED FOX

Andrew Matthews

G.S.O.H.

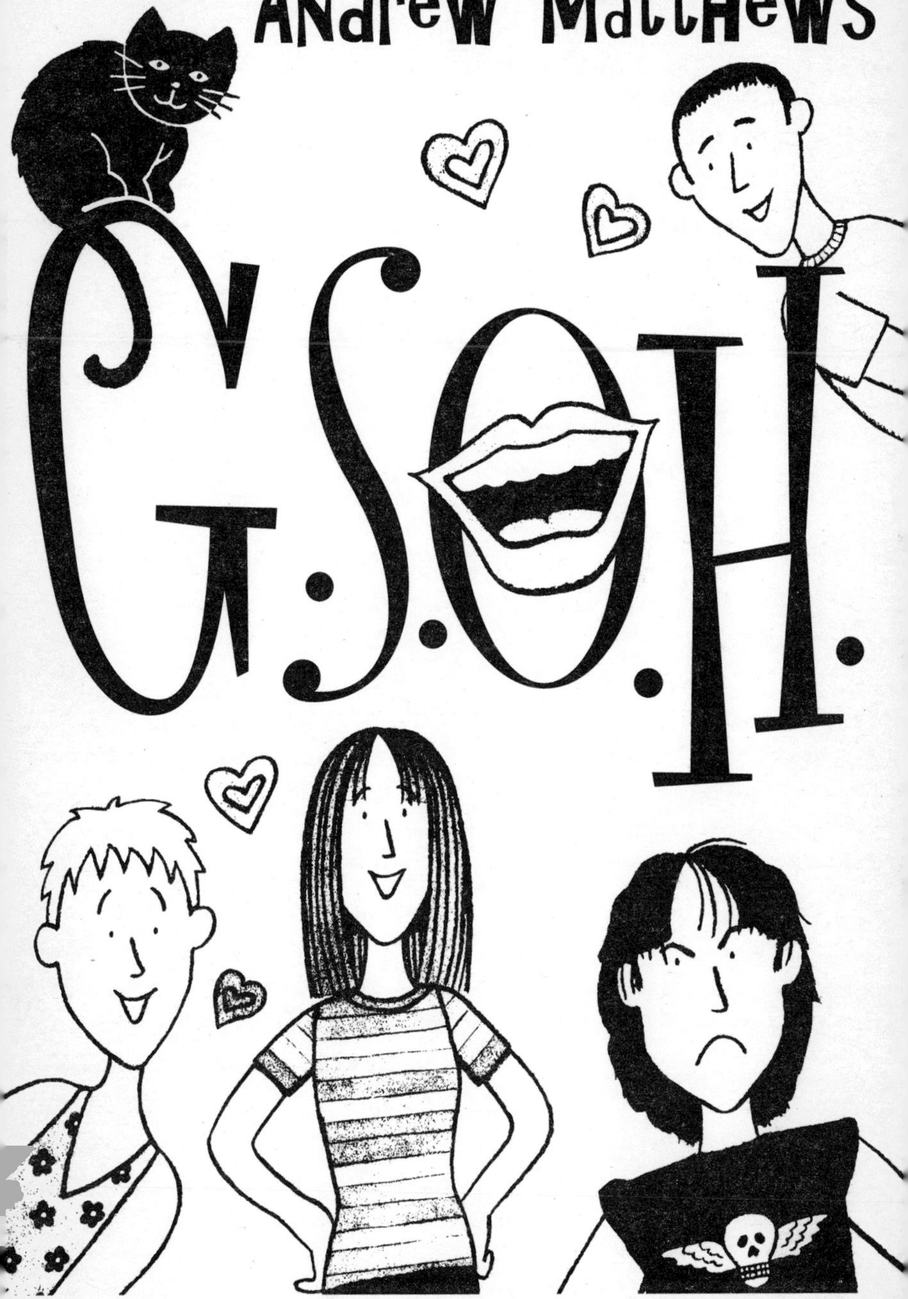

RED FOX

A Red Fox Book

Published by Random House Children's Books
20 Vauxhall Bridge Road, London SW1V 2SA

A division of The Random House Group Limited
London Melbourne Sydney Auckland
Johannesburg and agencies throughout the world

3 5 7 9 10 8 6 4

First published in Great Britain by
Red Fox Children's Books in 2001

Printed and bound in Great Britain by
Bookmarque Ltd. Croydon, Surrey.

Papers used by The Random House Group are natural, recyclable products
made from wood grown in sustainable forests. The manufacturing
processes conform to the environmental regulations
of the country of origin.

The Random House Group Limited Reg. No. 9540009

www.randomhouse.co.uk

ISBN 0 09 941389 2

To Pat and Liz
with love

'So it's come to this,' Katie thought. 'I'm fifteen years old, it's nearly the end of the summer holiday and the most exciting thing I can find to do is visit the library!'

Actually the library had its compensations, such as excellent air-conditioning.

Outside, the town was baking in late-August heat. People were walking around in shorts and shades, with stunned expressions on their faces. The air above the library car park shimmered like a mirage and the Tarmac had turned into black chewing gum.

Inside the library it was cool, but only as in 'not hot'.

Max ran his index finger down the columns printed on one of the back pages of the local newspaper and frowned.

'What does WLTM mean?' he asked Katie.

'Would like to meet.'

'Got it! Hey, how about this one? *Professional gent, 50, WLTM—*'

'Nah! Fifty's far too old. He has to be someone between thirty-five and forty, you know? Mature but not ancient.'

Max scanned the columns again and his eyes

lit up. 'Here we go! *Leo male, 40, WLTM Sagit-tarean female, 30+, to share cosmic vibes.*'

'Does it say anything about SOH?'

'What's that?'

'Sense of humour. It must say SOH or, even better, GSOH.'

'Good sense of humour?' Max guessed.

'Yup. It's the most important thing in a relationship. If couples can't have a laugh together, they row about stuff.'

'I wouldn't know,' said Max. 'I suppose that means a thirty-five-year-old guy keenly interested in women's clothing, who WLTM a sympathetic female for costume experimentation is totally out of the question?'

'Absolutely totally.'

'Or a male raver, thirty-four, searching for a groovy chick?'

'A groovy chick?' said Katie.

Max shrugged. 'Go figure.'

Something had been bothering Katie all afternoon. She hadn't been going to mention it, but her curiosity finally got the better of her. 'Max, did you borrow that T-shirt off your dad?'

The T-shirt was black, with a picture of a winged skull on the front. The winged skull had once been sparkling silver, but repeated washings had faded it to a murky grey.

'Certainly did!' Max said cheerfully. 'Classic, isn't it?'

'If you go for morbid, yeah.'

'*Morbid?*' said Max, blinking at Katie as if she'd just stepped out of a UFO.

Max was heavily into Seventies stuff. As well as the T-shirt he was wearing flared denim jeans, a belt with a massive buckle shaped like an amoeba and lime green flip-flops. He was currently listening to a lot of Boney-M and Abba.

Katie wasn't bothered much: Max's taste in clothes – or lack of it, depending on your point of view – had played a crucial role in their relationship. They'd been standing next to each other in the Infants' playground, Katie in a blue cardigan, Max in a pink pullover, and Bradley Wilkes had walked over to them and said, 'Huh? You're wrong!'

'Who is?' Katie said.

'You two. *Girls* are supposed to wear pink and *boys* are supposed to wear blue!'

Katie had given Bradley a look that would've burned holes through paper and said, 'Go play hide, Bradley.'

'What's that?'

'It's like hide-and-seek, only after you've hidden, nobody comes seeking you.'

Max had burst out laughing and that was that; he and Katie had been mates ever since.

Max sat back and peeled a lock of floppy brown hair off his forehead. 'Face it, Katie, your quest is doomed to failure. You're never going to find the right bloke. You'd better give up and stop wasting your time.'

3

'No chance! He's out there somewhere, I know he is. Sometimes I get this mental picture of what he looks like – kind eyes, grey streak in his hair, warm smile—'

'Dream on!' said Max.

Katie let her eyes drift over to the librarian who was on duty at the desk. She'd seen him loads of times, but had never considered his potential before. 'Hmm!' she thought. 'Thirty-something professional male, tall, slim, brown eyes, great smile WLTM—'

'Katie,' said Max, 'what are you doing?'

'Looking at him.'

'Who?'

'Mr Parker.'

'And Mr Parker would be?'

'The librarian over there.'

Max peered. 'What, *that* librarian over there?'

'Uh-huh.'

'How come you know his name?'

'Er, I read it on his lapel badge. I think I could be in with a chance.'

'Definitely not!' Max said, shaking his head. 'Bet you you're wrong.'

'How much?'

'Cappuccinos and caramel slices at Manconi's?'

'You're on!'

'Method A or Method B?'

'Method A. He's a librarian, isn't he?'

Max looked admiringly at Katie. 'The extent

4

of your deviousness never ceases to amaze me, you know that?'

'I amaze myself at times,' Katie said.

Method A involved the Indirect Approach. Ideally it would also have included an impressive-looking folder, but Katie hadn't had a chance to plan in advance, so she improvised by using the blank pages in her Filofax. As a matter of fact, all the pages in the Filofax were blank. It had been a present from Aunt Cath and Uncle Bryan. Katie had never used it because she figured she was already organised, but carried it around in her bag because it was too good to throw away, and besides, you never knew when a Filofax might come in handy – like now, for instance.

Katie sidled over to the desk, put on her bimbo air-head face, cleared her throat and said, 'Excuse me? Mr Parker?'

Mr Parker turned to look at her. 'Can I help you?'

'Ooh, I hope so! You see, I'm gathering data for a project that has to be handed in on the first day of next term, and I wondered if you'd mind answering a few questions.'

Mr Parker's eyes narrowed in suspicion. 'What sort of questions?'

'Nothing too personal. It's a socio-economic thing.'

Mr Parker needed convincing; Katie went in for the kill.

'I should have started on it ages ago, of course, but I'm terrible about leaving things to the last minute, and I wouldn't have had the cheek to ask you, but I'm really worried I won't finish it in time and I'll get a detention if I don't, which isn't a very good way to begin the new school year.'

Mr Parker's eyes softened: the old hapless female routine worked every time.

'All right.'

Katie made a show of scribbling in the Filofax. 'Well, first of all you're male, obviously, and your occupation?'

'Librarian,' Mr Parker said with a sigh.

'How old are you, Mr Parker?'

'Thirty-six.'

'And are you married at all?'

'Not even slightly.'

'So you're single?'

'I live with my partner.'

Bummer!

'How old is she, Mr Parker?'

Mr Parker stiffened. '*He's* twenty-nine.'

Katie snapped the Filofax shut. 'That's all, Mr Parker. Thank you very much for your time.'

Three steps away from the desk, the blush kicked in. By the time she got back to Max, Katie was glowing red.

'Strike out?' said Max.

'You set me up, you rat. You *knew*!'

'Knew what?'

6

'About Mr Parker!'

'What about him?'

Was that a smug smile playing around the corners of Max's mouth?

Katie couldn't tell, and decided to give him the benefit of the doubt. 'OK,' she said grudgingly. 'Manconi's is on me.'

2

Manconi's was as retro as Max, except that its target nostalgia era was the Nineteen-fifties. The chairs were made of plywood ovals with pointed ends, riveted to tubular metal frames; the tables were circular sheets of smoked glass. Behind the counter, the chromed espresso machines looked like the controls of a starship.

Katie ate the froth on top of her cappuccino with a spoon and was two-thirds of the way through her caramel slice before she noticed that Max hadn't touched his. He was slumped in his chair, staring at his reflection in the table, eyes as dead as a doll's.

'Something up, Max?'

'I'm not in the mood for caramel slices.'

Coming from Max, this was almost blasphemy. He was the Caramel Slice Kid and had been known to chug down four in one sitting. Katie was the person who knew because she'd been there at the time.

'Don't give me that, Max! What's wrong?'

'Not hungry.'

Katie had an awful feeling that she knew what was coming, but Max wasn't the cut-to-the-chase type. He needed coaxing; handling him demanded tact and sensitivity.

Katie said, 'If you don't tell me, right now, that caramel slice is going straight up your left nostril.'

Max wriggled his shoulders. Words came out of his mouth as reluctantly as back teeth. 'It just hit me what I was doing in the library. Like I was reading through the Lonely Hearts ads trying to help you out, and meanwhile my own love-life is a complete mess!'

'Max, you don't have a love-life.'

'Yes I do . . . in a way.'

'This is about Jasmine Walls, isn't it?'

Max didn't need to reply.

'I thought you were over that!'

'So did I,' Max said. 'But I bumped into her this morning and . . . I don't know, she's so— Like if you look at her, her eyes are green, but if you *really* look at her, they've got yellow bits in them – flakes of gold.'

'Please don't go there, Max! This caramel slice is sickly enough as it is. Where did you bump into her?'

'Well, I didn't do any bumping, exactly. I was sort of strolling past her house and—'

'What were you doing at her house? She lives on the other side of town from you!'

Max went defensive. 'I woke up early, I fancied a walk, next thing I know, there's Jasmine. I kind of smiled and said hello.'

'What did she say?'

9

'Nothing. I don't think she heard me. I was on the other side of the road, in a park, behind a tree.'

'Max, you were practically stalking the girl! Get some tickets to reality, will you?'

'I can't help it!'

'Yes you can. Get a grip! Jasmine Walls is not the girl for you.'

'Why?' Max said indignantly. 'Because a girl who looks like her could never be interested in a guy who looks like me? Because she's a radiant goddess and I'm an earthworm?'

'No,' Katie said. 'Because firstly, you can't seriously be in love with a girl whose name sounds like an interior-decoration scheme, and because secondly, she's going out with Jordan Stevens.'

Max snorted. 'That jerk! He doesn't deserve someone like Jasmine. I mean, take away Jordan's hunky looks, athletic build, wit and charm, and what have you got left? Mr Nobody!'

'But they're crazy about each other, Max! Jordan hung upside down to spray *Jaz 4 Jord* on that railway bridge.'

'I know, but . . .' Real pain emerged from the cover of Max's jokes. A tear rolled down his face and splashed on to the table, making a shape that was an exact replica of his belt buckle. 'When's my turn coming, Katie? When do I get the breaks?'

'It'll happen. Hang on in there. Be patient.

When the right girl comes along she'll be worth the wait.'

Max smiled through his tears. 'Thanks, Katie! If it hurts, stick a cliché on it – right?'

Katie thought, 'Male, fifteen, OK-looking, tragic dress-sense, WLTM understanding female to be gentle with him.'

Lonely Hearts columns, it seemed, were contagious.

Katie closed the front door and heaved a sigh of relief. The walk from the bus stop had been murder: air so thick it was like breathing fog, pavement burning up through the soles of her sandals, sun pounding on the top of her head. She grabbed a Dr Pepper from the fridge, went into the lounge to flop in front of the TV and stopped dead.

There was the little shrine Mum had hung above the fireplace: the portrait of Dad, taken by a professional photographer, then on the left the picture of him and Mum, and on the right the picture of the three of them. Mum and Dad were smiling, Katie was scowling. She didn't like the photographer because he treated her like a little girl – which she had been when the picture was taken.

Three months later, Dad's car had skidded on a patch of black ice, piled into a tree at the side of the road and killed him outright.

Nothing had ever been the same afterwards.

11

'This is down to you, Dad,' Katie murmured. 'If you hadn't been driving so fast—'

But she'd been through all that years ago: if he'd driven slower, if he'd left the house a few minutes earlier or later, if he'd stuck to the main road instead of taking a short cut – then the accident wouldn't have happened. It was more comforting to believe that Dad had been fated to die that day and there was no way that he could have avoided it, like if he'd stayed at home he would have dropped dead from a heart attack.

Katie had mourned for her father, accepted his death and put it behind her; but Mum hadn't. Mum was still grieving, and that was the problem. Mum was so devoted to Dad's memory that Katie was afraid she'd vanish altogether.

It couldn't be healthy, keeping his clothes hanging in the wardrobe, his slippers at the side of the bed, his shaving gear in the bathroom cabinet. He'd been dead almost five years, but Mum still acted like he was about to walk in at any minute. Katie had even caught Mum ironing one of his shirts.

Time after time Katie had tried to persuade her mother to have a clear-out, but Mum's reaction was always the same: 'I still love him. I'm still married to him. I can't throw him away.'

Mum was bright, pretty, funny and reasonably young, but she was wasting her life. She dressed like a granny: frumpy tweed suits for work, baggy sweatshirts and – ohmygod! – tracksuit bottoms at home. All she did was get up, go to work, eat and sleep. She wouldn't go out and have fun, she never tried to meet anyone new. There had to be a million unattached men Mum's age who'd leap at the chance to go out on a date with her, but Mum didn't want to know.

And it was driving Katie nuts.

Mum came home at six. She sagged against the doorway of the lounge, glanced at the photo of Dad and said, 'If I never have another day like today, it'll be too soon!'

'You work too hard,' said Katie.

'Too hard I can handle. It's when I'm asked to do the impossible that I have trouble.'

'You ought to relax more. Enjoy yourself a little!'

'I'm too busy to enjoy myself. How was your day?'

'Boring. I met up with Max. We hung.'

'Anywhere in particular?'

'The library.'

'Why the library?'

'We looked through the Lonely Hearts columns in the local rag to see if we could find you a boyfriend.'

Mum laughed; finding her a boyfriend was like a running joke between her and Katie. 'Any luck?'

'Almost. Had this great guy lined up, but it didn't work out.'

'Not to worry,' Mum said. 'Better luck next time!'

She had no idea how serious Katie was.

Katie thought, 'Thirty-something female, attractive, vivacious, WLTM male of same age with GSOH and . . .'

But she couldn't come up with the rest; GSOH was important, but it wasn't everything.

3

On the last Friday evening of the holiday Katie and Max went clubbing, decided to give The Red Airplane a try and lucked in because the bouncer on the door was Oscar.

Oscar's shoulders were wide enough to fill the shoulders of his dinner-jacket and his fists were like bags of walnuts, but he had a soft spot for Katie. He never asked to see her ID and had once let her stroke his goatee.

'Princess!' he said, beaming at Katie. 'Looking good.' Then he glanced at Max and frowned. 'Do the Style Police know about you, son?'

Max shoved his wraparound mirror-shades further up his nose and said, 'Haven't you heard? The Seventies are back. Retro is the new progressive.'

Oscar shrugged with one side of his mouth. 'If you say so. Nice shirt. Shame somebody's been sick over it.'

'It's paisley – a designer original!'

'Can't come in wearing that getup, son. You could give someone a migraine.'

Max prepared to object, which wasn't the way to handle Oscar.

Katie came to the rescue, batting her

eyelashes. 'Oh, go on, Oscar! If you don't let my friend in, I won't have anyone to dance with.'

'Stop before you break my heart! OK, inside – quick, before I change my mind. If I catch either of you with booze, you're out on your ear, right?'

Max sniffed disdainfully. 'As if! Alcohol is s-o-o Twentieth Century.'

The interior of The Red Airplane was black, the only red thing in the place being the papier-mâché aeroplane that hung above the dance floor. The bar in the entrance was relatively quiet, separated from the dance floor by two heavy-duty fire doors that acted as sound-proofing. Every time the doors opened, they let out a blast of music loud enough to register on the Richter scale.

Through the doors, the noise level was industrial strength. Lasers stabbed the dark-ness; strobes fluttered. Around the walls, banks of TV screens showed computer animations, clips of old cartoons and black-and-white films. Dancers twitched and bobbed like corks in a tide. The focus was the stage, from which two DJs dispensed a collage of twiddly synthesisers and a wailing gospel choir, held together by a pulsing Techno beat.

Katie and Max hit the floor. Max danced as if he had elastic bones, waving his hands like he was plaiting air into a rope. Katie had no idea of how she looked when she was dancing.

She surrendered herself to the music and let everything go – identity, anxieties and time disappeared into a black place.

After an hour they went to the bar to cool down and drink ridiculously overpriced cola.

Max took off his shades and showed Katie that the lenses were steamed up on the inside. 'It's like Singapore in there!' he said, fanning his face with his hand. 'If the humidity goes any higher, storm-clouds are going to form.'

And all at once Max had his own personal storm-cloud to deal with: Jasmine Walls emerged through the double doors, waved and started to walk over.

Katie felt Max go rigid.

'Oh no!' he groaned. 'I really don't need this.'

'Take it easy, Max.'

'I can't. It hurts.'

Max stood up when Jasmine reached the table, said, 'Hi! You can take my chair. Can't stop, I have to be . . . somewhere!' and scurried away before Katie could stop him.

Jasmine sat down with a sigh and wiped sweat off her forehead, managing to make the gesture look graceful.

'Where's Jordan?' asked Katie.

'In Florida, with his family. He gets back tomorrow.'

'So you're on your own?'

'I came with Gavin – Gavin Macey, you know?'

'And where's Gavin?'

'Dancing with Charmaine. I think they're going to get it together.'

'Again?' said Katie, boggling. 'How many times have they broken up now?'

'I lost count. Why did Max take off like that?'

'Guess.'

'He hasn't still got a thing for me, has he? I thought he was over that.'

'That was a crush. This time he thinks he's in love.'

Jasmine rolled her eyes. 'What is it with boys? Why are they so . . .? Why can't they . . .?'

'Exactly,' said Katie.

'Would you mind if I asked you something?'

'I won't know if I mind until after you've asked. What's it about?'

'Well, you and Max hang out together a lot, like you're really close, aren't you?'

'Uh-huh.'

'So have you and he ever?' Jasmine broke off, realising that her curiosity had got the better of her mouth.

'Once,' said Katie. 'It was before Christmas, when I was off with that flu bug? Max came over and we started talking about what it would be like to be an item. Then he snogged me to see if anything would happen.'

'And did it?'

'Kind of. Right in the middle of the snog we

18

burst out laughing and all this gunge came down my nose.'

'Eew, gross!'

'That pretty much did it for me and Max and romance. We figured our friendship was too important to get into boy–girl stuff.'

'I know what you mean!' said Jasmine. 'Sometimes I think that Jordy and I . . .'

She went into a long rap about her and Jordan, how they took each other for granted, how the magic had gradually worn off.

Katie pretended to listen, but her attention was elsewhere. She was watching Oscar. He was on his break, sipping lager at the bar. There was something vulnerable about him when he wasn't being a bouncer, kind of lost and sad.

'Mature, fit male,' Katie thought. 'WLTM kind, sympathetic female for lasting relationship.'

'And I'm not sure what I should do,' Jasmine concluded. 'What would you do, Katie?'

'Dump him and move on. Hey, how old would you say Oscar was?'

'Oscar the bouncer? Hard to tell. Forty?'

'I'd guess thirty-eight. He's not bad, is he?'

Jasmine's jaw dropped. 'You're interested in older men?'

'No, but I know a woman who ought to be. Mind my chair, will you? I'll be back in a minute.'

Katie sidled up to the bar, purse at the ready,

and stood next to Oscar. She gave him an exaggerated double-take and said, 'Oh, hi! I didn't see you there.'

'Should have,' said Oscar. 'There's enough of me.'

'And I bet it's all muscle. D'you work out?'

Oscar straightened his bow-tie and thrust out his chin. 'Try to keep fit, you know.'

'Does your wife take exercise as well?'

'I wouldn't know, we divorced ten years ago.'

'Have you got a girlfriend?'

Oscar raised an eyebrow. 'Here, you trying to come on to me or something?'

'No,' said Katie. 'I think you ought to take my mum out.'

Oscar nearly choked on his lager. 'You what?'

'You'd like her. She's really pretty – look!' Katie opened the back of her purse and fished out the holiday photo of Mum in Greece, lying on a sun-lounger in a one-piece swimming costume.

Oscar stared. 'That's your mum?'

'Yup.'

'Not your sister?'

'Nope. Her name's Jennifer. She's a widow and she doesn't go out anywhere except work. If you asked her for a date, you'd be doing her a favour.'

'Not backward about coming forward, are you?'

'I don't have time,' said Katie. 'I figure, you're nice, she's nice, so why not?'

Oscar laughed. 'Had me going there for a minute! You've got a lot to learn, princess.'

'No I don't. I've got the basics, the rest is improvisation. Pen?'

Oscar took a black felt-tip out of his inside pocket and handed it to Katie.

Katie wrote her phone number on a cardboard coaster. 'There you go! Give her a buzz, but don't call her Jenny, OK? She doesn't like it.'

'You're crazy!'

'Because I want my mum to have a life? What's crazy about that?'

'I'm a total stranger, for starters.'

'But you won't be strangers once you get to know each other, will you?'

Oscar looked like he was searching for an answer that wasn't there; Katie wondered why logic always did that to people.

Max was another logic-free zone. He reappeared shortly after Jasmine disappeared, wearing his puppy-face – wistful eyes and drooping mouth.

'Where did you get to?' Katie demanded.

'I took a walk. I couldn't handle being with her.'

'You're deeply sad.'

'Tell me about it.'

'Running away isn't the answer to anything.'

'That depends on what the question is. If I'd stuck around, I would've seen that Jasmine wasn't interested and then I wouldn't have had a hope. This way is better.'

'What way?'

'Keeping her at a distance.' Max's eyes went starry. 'I have this fantasy that Jasmine and I will bump into each other at the right time in the right place, and we'll have *the* conversation, the one that makes her realise that we're meant to be together.'

'Excuse me? If you keep her at a distance, how will you have the conversation?'

'I'll wait for destiny to lend a hand,' Max said airily.

'You don't wait for destiny, Max! You go out and *make* it happen. You know your problem? You're enjoying yourself. I mean, you actually *like* eating your heart out. If you had a relationship with Jasmine, it wouldn't be anywhere near as good as the one in your head.'

'That's the whole point!' said Max. 'I can have a beautiful dream or a disappointing reality. No contest, is there?'

Katie wasn't certain whether to say yes or no to this, so instead she told Max about Oscar.

Max was alarmed. 'Is that a good idea?'

'Isn't it?'

'How will your mum react?'

'She'll be cool with it. She likes surprises.'

'Katie, there are surprises, and then there are shocks,' Max pointed out.

'Mum needs a shock! She's dug herself so deep in a hole, she's practically buried.'

'And you want to shock her so she jumps out?'

'Right.'

Max nodded. 'It'll never work,' he said.

4

Katie woke up on Sunday morning and there was school, a tight band of anxiety in the pit of her stomach. All the things she'd been putting off thinking about over the summer came crashing down on her like a tidal wave. Going into Year Ten meant the start of GCSE courses, new subjects, new sets, new teachers. Last term Katie had clocked the crowds of Year Elevens filing into the Sports Hall to take their exams. They'd looked shell-shocked, pale and hollow-eyed, laughing too long and too loudly. Before too long Katie would be just like them and she wasn't looking forward to it. Being a teenager was a pain, but what you had to go through to grow up really sucked.

In the shower, Katie tried to think positive. At least the first day of term would be short: only Year Seven had to attend school in the morning; the other years didn't have to turn up until after lunch. That would leave Katie with an awkward few hours when she wouldn't be on holiday any more, but she wouldn't be back at school yet. It figured; she seemed to spend most of her time in between things.

Cleo paced up and down the bathroom, warbling and chirruping. Cleo was an old black cat, savvy about humans and their ways, but she'd never understood why they drenched themselves in water every morning.

Katie stepped out of the cubicle and wrapped herself in a towel. 'Stop nagging!' she told Cleo. 'If you think showers are crazy, you ought to see what goes on at school.'

Cleo purred, happy that at last Katie had shown the sense to come in out of the rain.

Downstairs it was very Sunday morning: Mum in the lounge, drinking coffee as she read the paper; next door's lawnmower whining; the theme tune to The Archers playing faintly on a distant radio. Katie grabbed a bowl of cereal and went to join Mum. She didn't talk to Mum and Mum didn't talk to her. They sat in a companionable silence that made words unnecessary.

Then Mum spoiled it by saying, 'Are you all set for tomorrow?'

'No.'

'I picked up your uniform from the cleaner's yesterday. It's hanging—'

'On the spare-bedroom door. I know.'

'You must be looking forward to going back.'

'Huh?'

'You've been at a loose end this past week.'

'Being at a loose end is better than putting my head in a noose!'

Mum looked up from her paper. 'That bad?'

'Worse. Next Sunday I'll be waist-deep in assignments.'

'You'll cope. You always do.'

Which was true, but there were times when Katie felt that there ought to be more to existence than coping.

'You'll see all your friends again,' Mum went on.

'What friends – Max?'

'You must have more friends than Max.'

'Must I? There are people I get on with, but they're not exactly friends.'

Mum turned a page. 'It'll be boys next,' she said.

'Then they'll have to be beamed down from another planet. The boys in my year are spotty, nerdy or taken.'

'Really?' said Mum, meaning, 'Not really.'

'Some of them are living proof that *homo sapiens* bred with Neanderthals.'

'You shouldn't be so critical.'

'I'm not critical, I've got high standards. Just because my body is a mass of raging hormones doesn't mean I'm about to fling myself at the first male who shows an interest.'

'Perhaps David will ask you out again.'

Katie froze. 'Don't even go there!' she growled.

It was possibly her most embarrassing moment. Last Easter, after weeks of sighing loudly every time Katie passed him in the corridor, Dave Michaels had arrived tongue-tied and blushing on the doorstep, clutching a bunch of flowers. It took him five stammering minutes to say what he had to say, and he left disappointed, trailing the flowers behind him.

'He seemed a nice enough boy,' Mum said, pushing it.

'I don't like nice boys!'

'Then what sort of boys *do* you like?'

Interesting question. Handsome wouldn't hurt; GSOH, natch. Katie was still thinking about it when the phone rang.

Mum didn't stir.

'I'll get that, shall I?' said Katie.

'Would you mind, love? If it's somebody from work, tell them I'm in the bath and take a message.'

'Why not let the answering machine take the message?'

'Because it might be important.'

Katie swallowed the question about how if it might be important, why didn't Mum answer it herself, and went into the hall.

'Hello?'

'Hello. Is that Jennifer?'

Oscar's voice. Katie was excited to hear it, because it meant that her plan was working out.

'It's Katie.'

'Who?'

'Princess. Hang on.'

Katie returned to the lounge. 'It's for you.'

Mum pulled a face. 'Is it desperate?'

'Could be.'

Katie perched on the arm of the chair nearest

the door, so that she could earwig without being seen. It was going to work. Mum would be blown away by Oscar's romantic impulsiveness and would accept his offer of a date at once.

Only Mum's half of the conversation didn't sound promising. She said, 'I'm sorry?' and 'Who?' and, after a longish silence, 'How did you obtain this number?' There was a longer silence before Mum said, 'She did *what*?'

Katie didn't listen to the rest. She slumped into the chair and waited for the ten-tonne weight to drop on her head.

Mum was worse than angry – she acted dismayed, like Katie had let her down. Katie hated having guilt trips laid on her, especially when she'd done something to deserve it.

'That was Oscar,' Mum said as she entered the lounge. 'Apparently you two know each other.'

'Um, yeah.'

'He claims that you gave him our phone number last night.'

'Did I?' Katie said, trying to force herself down the back of the chair.

'Yes. He tells me that you encouraged him to ask me out.'

'I did?'

'Yes.'

'And did he?'

'Yes.'

'I take it the answer was no.'

Mum lowered herself on to the sofa and stared at Katie as though she didn't recognise her. 'Whatever were you thinking of?'

'That you ought to go out more.'

'With a *bouncer*?'

'Oscar's a good guy.'

'I don't care if he's St Francis of Assissi! You had no right to meddle with my private affairs, Katie. Do I meddle with yours?'

'All the time.'

'That's different, I'm your mother. I can't believe that you'd be so irresponsible as to give our phone number to any Tom, Dick or Harry.'

'I didn't. I gave it to Oscar.'

Mum was teetering on the brink of losing her temper. She took a deep, calming breath and said, 'I don't know what was going through your mind and, to be honest, I'd prefer not to. I can decide what's right for me without any help from you, thanks very much.'

'Message received. Am I grounded?'

'No, we're going to forget that this ever happened – but first you have to promise me that you won't do anything like this again.'

Katie didn't reply.

'Promise!' Mum insisted.

'I promise,' mumbled Katie. She didn't have a problem with it, because she was only promising not to hand out Mum's phone number to any more bouncers. That's where Katie thought she'd gone wrong – Mum deserved someone classier.

5

Next day, Katie called for Max and they walked to school together. It was strange seeing Max in uniform again; it made him look like a schoolkid.

'This is it!' he declared. 'The future begins right here. Education is the key to success and I'm going to grab every chance I get with both hands.'

'Scared?' said Katie.

'Terrified. Why did they put us in top sets for everything, Katie? You have to work in top sets.'

'It's a punishment for being bright.'

'I'm having an attack of exam nerves.'

'But your GCSE courses haven't started yet.'

'Why wait?' Max said gloomily.

They turned into Church Lane and joined the stream of pupils headed for the school gates. On campus the staff were out in force, chivvying people along; they didn't seem thrilled about the start of term either.

'Ah, school!' said Max. 'How I've missed it.'

'How have you missed it?'

'Not at all.'

As they passed the bike sheds, Katie and Max met Mr Davis, their form tutor.

'Katie!' said Mr Davis. 'Just the person I was hoping to run into.'

'Lucky for her you're not in your car, sir,' said Max.

Mr Davis smiled mirthlessly. 'I see the summer vacation has done nothing to improve your sense of humour, Max. Shame. Katie, I want you to do something for me.'

'Sir?' Katie said.

'Don't go to the form room when the bell rings. Wait for me in reception. I'll meet you there after the staff meeting.'

'Why?'

Mr Davis didn't answer because he was distracted by a Year Eight. 'Tod, do up your tie!' he snapped. 'Tuck in your shirt, tie up your shoelaces, lose the nose-studs and Walkman, and wash the fake tattoos off the backs of your hands!'

Mr Davis seemed to be enjoying himself so much that Katie didn't like to interrupt him. She and Max walked off.

'Outstanding!' said Katie. 'I'm back two minutes and I'm in trouble already.'

'You don't know you're in trouble.'

'No – so why does Mr Davis want to see me in reception?'

'Probably because you're in trouble.'

'I can't be! I haven't done anything.'

'Since when did not doing anything stop someone from being in trouble with a teacher?'

'Good point,' said Katie.

Katie wasn't the only one waiting in reception. A girl was seated in one of the chairs near the trophy cabinet. She had short blonde hair and a quirkily attractive face: big blue eyes, slightly turned-up nose, pointed chin. Her uniform and school bag were brand new. She looked nervous and embarrassed.

Katie thought, 'Terrified female, fifteen, WLTM friendly face,' sat in the empty chair next to the girl and said, 'First day?'

The girl's mouth pulled down at the corners. 'Does it show?'

''Fraid so. Where are you from?'

'Woking. Dad changed jobs. We moved here a fortnight ago. What's this place like?'

'OK-ish. The teachers aren't bad. Most of the kids are human.'

The girl grinned. 'Sounds like my last school. I'm Briony.'

'Katie.'

'I like your hair.'

'You can have it if you want. I only keep it so's not to be bald.'

Briony laughed, and all of a sudden she and Katie were getting on. They chatted, made each other giggle. Briony said that she needed a giggle – before the move she'd had to end a promising relationship with a guy called Phil.

'We promised to be in touch and stay friends, but it won't be the same. I blame my dad. All he cares about is his career.'

'What does he do?'

Briony lowered her eyes, blushed and mumbled something that Katie didn't catch.

Mr Davis materialised out of nowhere and said, 'So you two have already made yourselves acquainted? Excellent. Briony is joining our form and I want you to keep an eye on her, Katie. Show her the ropes.'

'Ropes?'

'Metaphorically speaking. Shall we go? Mustn't keep the rest of Nine L waiting.'

'Ten L,' said Katie.

'Of course! I was forgetting,' Mr Davis said. 'It seems only yesterday that you were Seven L. How time flies when one's having fun.'

Registration was as chaotic as ever. Mr Davis issued Ten L with homework logs and ran through glitches in the timetable.

'As some of you are doubtless aware, Miss Hargreaves left unexpectedly at the end of the summer term . . .'

Goss was that she'd run off to Provence with an OFSTED inspector.

'. . . and as a result, the top English set will be taught by Mr Lucas.'

'Is he new, sir?' someone called out.

'Yes, so new that we haven't finished unwrapping him yet. And there's been a room change. Those of you who do Music on Thursday morning will go to the Art Suite for lessons. Those of you with Art will go to the Music Suite. This is a temporary measure and will only apply until the History Suite has been refurbished so that a Computer Suite can be installed. Are you all clear about that?'

'No!' chorused Ten L.

'Good,' said Mr Davis. 'This is going to be a tough year for you at first, but I think you'll find that it gets worse as it goes on. If any of you feel that you're having problems, no matter how small, please don't hesitate to leave me alone. I have problems of my own.'

The bell rang. Overhead, chairs scraped and feet thundered.

'Have a nice day now!' Mr Davis said.

Maths and French: textbooks, exercise books, folders, worksheets and pep-talks. Katie let it wash over her and kept an eye on Briony, like Mr Davis had told her to. Lots of eyes were being kept on Briony, particularly boys' eyes. Not Max though; he had his head down so low that Katie was afraid he might nod off.

'Wake up, Max!' she muttered.

'I am awake.'

'Could have fooled me.'

'I was thinking. There's a law against thinking?'

'No, but it's a waste of time to do it at school.'

Max glared. Something had been rattling his cage all afternoon, and Katie was dying to know what, but it would have to wait. The French teacher, Mrs Wilkie, didn't take kindly to private conversations during her lessons, and when she gave someone a telling-off she used a voice that could strip paint.

Last bell sounded. Katie, Max and Briony left the French Suite and went outside. Right on cue, the dark cloud hanging over the school dropped a thin veil of drizzle.

'Congratulations, you made it!' Katie said to Briony. 'How was it for you?'

'The earth didn't move, but it was all right.'

Katie waited for Max to come in with some crack, but he didn't. He stared at the drizzle.

'Where d'you live, Briony?' Katie asked.

'Kingfisher Drive.'

'That's on our way. We'll walk with you.'

Max shot Katie an annoyed look.

Briony shuffled her feet. 'Um, actually, I have to wait for my dad to pick me up.'

'Then we'll wait with you.'

Briony wasn't taken with this suggestion. 'No, don't, please! I'll be fine. He shouldn't be long. Thanks for taking care of me.'

'No worries. See you tomorrow.'

'Want to swap phone numbers? We could ring each other up for a chat.'

'As opposed to?' said Max.

Briony frowned. 'I'm sorry?'

'When people ring each other, it's generally for a chat, isn't it?'

'Ignore Mr Grumpy,' said Katie. 'He's having a bad-hormone day.'

Max was certainly having a bad-something day. While she and Briony exchanged numbers, Katie could feel him giving off waves of – what – anger, hostility? Katie couldn't understand it.

Katie and Max left Briony at Main Entrance and strolled down Church Lane.

'Cute girl!' said Katie.

'Mm.'

'I think she's going to be a mate.'

'Oh.'

'What does that mean?'

'It means *oh*.'

'What's the matter, don't you like her? You hardly said a word to her, and when you did it was sarcastic.'

'I don't like or dislike her. I couldn't think what to say to her.'

'You could've made an effort.'

'Why?'

'To be friendly! It was her first day at this school. That's a big deal, Max! What's wrong with you?'

'Nothing.'

'Oh, sure!'

They walked three paces in silence, then Max said, 'Katie, d'you ever get that thing where you meet someone and it's like you met them before, or dreamed about them, and you know straight off that something's going to happen between you that will turn your whole life around?'

'No.'

'Me neither,' said Max. 'I wonder what it feels like?'

6

Max was in no mood to invite Katie in for their usual post-school natter over a cup of tea, so she left him to stew and carried on home. She rescued the morning mail – all Mum's, nobody ever wrote to Katie – and put it next to the phone on the hall table, ready for Mum to pick up when she came in. Then she went upstairs to her bedroom to unload her textbooks and folders, and copy her timetable into her home-work log.

It would have been easy if Cleo hadn't decided to help by standing on the log and rubbing her whiskers against Katie's pen, purring loudly. They came to a compromise: Katie shifted Cleo on to her lap; Cleo settled down and demonstrated her love by occasion-ally needling Katie's thighs with her claws. As a result the final draft of Katie's timetable looked wonky in places but it was legible, which was the main thing. Katie wasn't fussed, figuring that neat presentation was a sign of a person who didn't have anything more interesting to do.

As soon as the phone rang, Cleo jumped clear. Katie hurried downstairs, grumbling to herself. She really *had* to get it together to nag Mum into having an extension installed.

'Hello?'

'Hi, Katie! It's Briony. Look, I'm sorry about after school. I wouldn't want you to think I was being huffy or anything.'

'No worries.'

'It's my dad. He checks out people I know by grilling them. It's incredibly embarrassing. I didn't want him to give you any grief.'

'Overprotective, huh?'

'Too right! Since Mum died, he's tried to be a father *and* a mother. When he can't get the balance right, he turns into a Nazi.'

Katie caught her breath. 'Your mum died?'

'Nearly five years ago.'

'Oh wow! Unreal!'

There was a puzzled pause before Briony said, 'Full marks for originality, Katie. Most people say something about being sorry.'

'I am sorry, but it *is* unreal. My dad died five years ago.'

'Really?'

'Kind of spooky, isn't it? Mr Davis tells me to look after you, and it turns out that we're both in single-parent families.'

'That's probably why he did it. Teachers are sneaky that way.'

For the next fifteen minutes, Katie and Briony compared parental notes.

'Sounds like you've got the better deal,'

Briony said ruefully. 'My dad doesn't negotiate with me, he yells.'

'Yeah, but my mum *explains* when I've done something wrong. That can be a pain too. She treats me as an adult. I keep telling her that I'm a teenager and teenagers are *supposed* to screw up, but she won't have it.'

'Parents, hey? It's a good job they've got us to put them straight, or they'd make a mess of everything.' Briony's voice became cautious. 'Is Max a good friend of yours?'

'The best!'

'He's a bit withdrawn, isn't he?'

'Max? You have to be joking! The guy has no off switch.'

'He was quiet this afternoon. Was it because of me?'

Katie had to think quickly. 'I doubt if it registered you were there. Max World is a pretty weird place. He has it bad for Jasmine Walls, Year Ten Goddess. Jasmine doesn't want to know. It makes him broody.'

'Does she give him a hard time?'

'*Max* gives Max a hard time. Jasmine wouldn't deliberately hurt his feelings. She's a Babe, but she's nice. You know, considerate, sensitive, intelligent—'

'Don't you just hate people who have everything? There was this girl in my old school who—'

Briony was interrupted by an irate male voice shouting, 'Are you intending to spend

40

the entire evening on the phone, Briony? Do the words *telephone* and *bill* sound at all familiar?'

'Oops!' said Katie. 'Was that the Big Bad Parent?'

'Uh-huh. Have to go now. Talk to you tomorrow.'

Katie had hoped that Briony wouldn't have noticed Max's attitude towards her. No luck there then, and Katie could see problems looming. The only explanation for Max's behaviour was that he'd taken an instant dislike to Briony, and if Briony was going to be a friend, Katie had to find a way of overcoming it.

'It would be good if everybody you liked, liked one another,' Katie thought.

But when had life ever been that straightforward?

Mum came into the kitchen, where Katie was preparing dinner, chopping tomatoes and onions.

'What was school like?' Mum asked.

'A load of buildings with teachers and kids in them. How was work?'

'Like being put through a food processor.' Mum shuddered. 'I had Mike Livingstone sniffing round again.'

'Is that the slimeball who tried it on with you at the Christmas party?'

'The same. I feel sorry for him in a way. He

can't have any friends, or they'd tell him about his aftershave. It makes my eyes water. Move over, I'll give you a hand.'

'Suddenly I'm a five-year-old who's not allowed to play with sharp things? There's a special way of cutting up tomatoes that only mummies know?'

'Why do teenagers talk like that?'

'Like what?'

'Like this?' said Mum. 'Like every sentence is a question? Is it because they all watch "Neighbours"?'

'Mum, nobody watches "Neighbours" any more.'

'Don't they?' Mum shook her head. 'Things change so quickly that I can't keep up any more. That's what happens to you when you get old.'

'Thirty-eight isn't old!'

'It's nearly forty.'

'You're not old! You're out of touch because all you do is work. If you—'

'Please, Katie. Let's not go down that road.'

Katie knew that if she said another word, Mum would remind her about Oscar.

7

Tuesday, lesson four, the top English set gathered outside the room where Mr Lucas was about to teach them for the first time. They were feeling slightly nervous because he was an unknown quantity.

'I bet he's the Teacher from Hell,' said Max. 'One of those steely-haired, sadistic, cynical types who's on a mission to make teenagers' lives a misery.'

'Sounds right up your street,' said Katie. 'I bet he's young and keen.'

'In your dreams! If he was young and keen he'd be in a more highly-paid job than teaching.'

Katie turned to Briony. 'How about you, Bri?'

'Sorry?'

'What do you think Mr Lucas will be like?'

Briony seemed as startled as a fox at a hunt ball.

'I, er, expect he'll be, um, like a teacher.'

Katie didn't know why Briony was so bugged, and was about to put it down to Max, when a hunk walked up to her.

'Hi, Katie!'

Katie blinked. It took her a while but eventually, underneath the great haircut-and-dye job and mahogany tan, she saw that the hunk was Dave Michaels.

'*Dave*?' she squeaked. 'What happened to you?'

Dave laughed, white teeth flashing in his tanned face. 'Two weeks in Corfu and a hairdresser. How was your summer?'

'It sort of started out at the beginning and finished at the end. What made you . . .?' Katie pointed at her head.

'Change of attitude, change of image,' said Dave. 'Look, I have to get going. Nice talking to you, Katie. Catch you again some time, yeah?'

'Yeah.'

Dave disappeared in the flow of pupils leaving the English Suite.

'Katie, put your tongue and eyeballs back in,' said Max.

'But that was Dave Michaels! He used to be . . . and now he's . . .'

'People change.'

'Sure, but usually for the worse.'

'He wanted to impress – that's why he made a point of talking to you. He wanted to show that he's laid your ghost.'

'Shame he didn't wait until after I was dead.'

Katie felt cheated. She'd been Dave's first Big Crush and had given him his first taste of rejection and heartache. Now he was fanciable, some other girl was going to reap the benefit.

Max could tell what Katie was thinking.

'Ask me what's the most difficult thing in comedy.'

'What's the mo—?'

'Timing,' said Max.

He was right: when you got your timing wrong, it was a total bummer.

Mr Lucas was tall – well, above average height – dark, except for a sprinkling of grey hairs, and handsome in a craggy, older-man, Harrison Fordish kind of way. The twinkle in his grey eyes hinted at a sense of humour, but the set of his mouth suggested that he could be stern if he needed to be. His opening speech to the class confirmed both impressions.

'A few ground rules before we get started, Year Ten. You want good grades and I want to help you to achieve them. Unfortunately, this is going to involve you in a lot of hard work which you're not always going to feel like doing. You're going to be under pressure from other subjects as well. I'm a reasonable man, so if you know you're going to miss a deadline, come and see me to negotiate a later date. Miss that later date, and you'll discover that I can be as unreasonable and objectionable as any other teacher. Questions?'

Not a hand was raised.

'Then let me ask you one. You've been studying English for most of your lives – what is it?'

A few hands: English was a language, used for the communication of thoughts, ideas, emotions and information. Mr Lucas wrote key points on the whiteboard.

'And where does English come from?'

Only one hand this time – Max's.

'Er, England?'

Mr Lucas was away, shooting off ideas. It was difficult not to catch his enthusiasm. The lesson was more like joining in a game than being taught.

English, it turned out, was a branch of German mixed with Celtic, Latin, Norwegian and a big dollop of Norman French after 1066. A lot of everyday words – such as bungalow, sherbet and typhoon – had been filched from other languages.

'So English is a hotchpotch?' someone commented.

'Think of it as a treasure chest,' said Mr Lucas. 'Let's select a single gem and hold it up to the light.' He wrote *Beauty* on the board. 'I want you to write a single sentence about beauty for next lesson. It can be a quotation from a poem or song, or a dictionary definition, I don't mind, but I expect you all to write something. I'm going to pick people at random to read out their sentences, and then we'll use them as the basis for a discussion.'

The bell rang.

Completely unexpectedly, Mr Lucas said, 'Thank you for being gentle with me, Year Ten.

I was apprehensive about meeting you, but that was fun!' and he gave the class a smile that made everybody glow.

English was followed by lunch. Katie, Max and Briony stood in line in the cafeteria. Katie carried her tray to an empty table; Max sat opposite her.

Briony dithered and took a half-step towards another table.

'Where are you going, Bri?' said Katie.

'Over there.'

'Why?'

'I thought you and Max might want to—'

'Huh? Come sit with us!'

'Are you sure you don't mind?' said Briony, looking straight at Max.

Max shrugged; Briony sat down.

Katie had to do something about Briony and Max. At the moment, the tension between them was tighter than the film-wrap on a video cassette. If she could only find a topic of conversation that would bring the three of them together . . .

'Don't look now, Katie,' Max said out of the corner of his mouth, 'but Dave Michaels is staring this way.'

'He is?'

'I think he's hoping for some quality eye-contact.'

Katie wouldn't have minded obliging him, but the Briony/Max situation was top of her list.

'Wasn't Mr Lucas brilliant?' she said. 'He got the whole class going. He certainly has the right stuff, doesn't he?'

Max leaned back in his chair; Briony kept her eyes on her plate and hunched her shoulders to make herself as small as possible.

'The Mr Lucas Show?' said Max. 'It was just an act.'

'Yeah, but it was a class act.'

'He won't be able to keep up the pace. Give him a week and he'll be as boring as the rest of the teachers.'

'I wouldn't be so sure. What d'you reckon, Bri?'

'Er, actually, he's my dad,' Briony said.

'What?'

'Mr Lucas is my father.'

Katie was taken off-balance. 'Is that right? I guess that explains why you've both got the same surname.'

Which was a mega-dumb thing to say, but Katie hadn't made the connection before.

'That's rough!' Max said sympathetically. 'Doesn't the school have a policy about staff not teaching their own children?'

'There was no way round it,' said Briony. 'The Head of English wanted Da— Mr Lucas to teach the top set, and Dad didn't want to put me in a lower set, so we're stuck with each other. He's Mr Lucas at school and Dad at home.'

'That's a bit schizophrenic, isn't it?'

'It certainly is.' Briony's eyes were pleading. 'I'd appreciate it if you didn't spread it around too much.'

Katie paused to consider what it would be like to be taught by a parent – nightmare! You'd get bawled out for everything twice.

'Is he as intense at home as he is in the classroom?' said Max.

'Pretty much.'

'How d'you handle it?'

'With difficulty,' Briony said.

Dave passed, lugging his tray over to the scraps-bin. When he emptied his plate into it, he glanced at Katie's table and Katie caught his eye.

Dave grinned at her.

What was that fluttering in Katie's chest, and why did she feel giddy?

By the end of the day, Katie was whacked. Her eyelids kept trying to close through lesson six, and on the way home she lurched along like a zombie.

The phone rang as soon as she closed the front door. Katie wasn't sure she could string two words together and thought about leaving the call for the answering-machine, but in the end she couldn't resist.

'Hello?'

'Katie? It's Dave.'

Katie was lost for words.

'Dave Michaels?' Dave said helpfully.

'Dave! Hi, how you doing?'

'Fine. Is this a good time to call – you're not too busy, are you?'

'No. All I have to do is think about beauty.'

'Sorry?'

'Doesn't matter. School stuff.'

Silence.

Dave obviously needed assistance, so Katie said, 'Did you ring me about anything in particular, or is this a social call?'

'I wanted to ask you something.'

'Ask away.'

Cleo emerged from the lounge, sat on the hall carpet and stared in amazement.

Katie looked down at herself and saw why: she was lacing the phone-lead between her fingers, and her legs were twisted together like a corkscrew.

'You're probably going to think I've got a nerve asking you this, especially after – well, Easter and everything . . . but . . .'

'Y-e-s?'

'I was wondering . . .'

'Y-e-s?'

'That girl who was sitting with you and Max at lunch-time. You wouldn't happen to know her name, would you?'

Katie thought, 'Oh, great! This is just great!'

8

Wednesday started with a problem and went rapidly downhill. The problem was what to do about Dave and Briony. Katie wanted to talk it over with Max, but since he got prickly whenever she mentioned Briony, she thought the roundabout approach would be best.

As they were walking up Church Lane, she said, 'Max, if you knew someone fancied somebody, and the person they fancied didn't know, would you tell them, or would that be like sticking your nose in? Only, if you didn't tell them, the person who fancied them might try to do something about it, and if the person they fancied didn't fancy them, their feelings would get hurt. But if the person they fancied told you they didn't fancy them, you could—'

'You lost me,' said Max.

'Where?'

'After you said *Max*. Run it past me again, but speak English this time, OK? Who's being fancied?'

'Briony.'

Max's mouth screwed up tighter than a cat's bottom.

'Oh. Who's doing the fancying?'

'Dave Michaels.'

'Oh.'

'Tricky, isn't it?'

'Why?'

'Well, you know . . . because . . .'

'You fancy Dave yourself?'

'No way! I don't fancy Dave in the slightest and he doesn't fancy me. We're like – been there, done that.'

'Makes perfect sense, doesn't it?' Max said bitterly. 'You can just see them together. Dave and Briony, they were made for each other – like Barbie and Ken. If you came up with the right songs, you could turn them into a hit musical!'

'Why are you angry?'

'I'm not.'

'You sound angry.'

'That's not anger, it's jealousy. I'm jealous of anybody who's happier than I am. Everybody's getting it together except me. What's so wrong with me?'

'Apart from the coming on too strong, the naff clothes and the smart mouth? Not a thing.'

'You forgot my lack of confidence – what smart mouth?'

'Yours! You're the Put-down King, Max. People find that pretty intimidating, you know?'

'Hark who's talking!'

'Huh?'

'Loads of guys are dying to ask you out, but

they don't have the nerve. You're Katie Drew, Glacier Girl, beautiful but aloof.'

Katie jabbed Max with her elbow.

'Beautiful – me? Get out of here! You only think that because you've known me so long that I've grown on you.'

'That's not true. If I didn't know you at all, I'd still think you were beautiful. As a matter of fact, if we'd never met I'd be in love with you.'

They were on campus by now, and Katie was still trying to get her head around how you could possibly be in love with someone you hadn't met, when Liz Ricks came scurrying over. Liz was tall, wore too much mascara and was Goss Central.

'Heard the latest?'

'No, but I'm about to,' said Katie.

Liz leaned in close, eyelashes thrashing like spiders' legs.

'Jasmine Walls broke up with Jordan Stevens last night. It was a mutual agreement. They decided things weren't leading anywhere, and that they'd be happier as friends. Jasmine's keeping her options open, but there's a strong possibility that Jordan will make a move on Louise Walker this weekend.'

'Are you sure?' said Max.

Liz gave him a withering look.

'Of course I'm sure! Jasmine rang Helen last night, Helen rang Donna and Donna rang me. You think I'd spread a *rumour*?'

Max didn't answer; he went in on himself.

Katie guessed it was because he had a lot to think about.

Like Katie, the morning couldn't make up its mind. The heat wave had well and truly broken and the weather was vague and misty, but at lunch-time the clouds cleared, the mist evaporated and Katie came to a decision.

Much as she regretted it, she'd blown her chance with Dave. If she'd known at Easter what he was going to look like in September, things might have been different, but she hadn't and they weren't. So, Dave and Briony – why not? At least helping them get together would give Katie the chance to do the noble thing and lend True Love a hand.

The decision made lunch awkward. Max was deep in a moody silence, Katie was waiting for the right moment to tell Briony about Dave, and Briony was caught in the middle, wondering why Max and Katie were on edge. Her attempt at conversation was like trying to start a car with a flat battery.

'D'you think it'll stay sunny this afternoon?'

'Maybe,' said Max.

'I hope it does. I'm fed up with grey skies and drizzle.'

Briony was gabbling, winding herself in deeper.

Katie rescued her by saying, 'Jasmine just came in, Max.'

Max turned to look, turned back and shrugged.

'She looks miserable, sitting on her own,' said Katie. 'Why don't you go cheer her up?'

'Not in the mood.' Max stood up, scraping his chair back. 'I'm going for a walk. I need some space.'

Briony watched Max leave the cafeteria.

'He's suffering, isn't he?' she said.

'He's wallowing. Max doesn't believe in happiness. He says that misery lasts longer, so it's more dependable.'

'That's a pity! Max is—'

Katie jumped right in.

'I know someone who fancies you.'

Briony's face went from shocked to puzzled, from puzzled to shiny-eyed and hopeful.

'You *do*?'

'Uh-huh. Dave Michaels. The hunk I was talking to before English? Him.'

The light in Briony's eyes died.

'Oh.'

'He rang me up last night and asked about you. Seems keen. I think he's working himself up to asking you out.'

'I hope he doesn't!' Briony said, squirming in her chair. 'I hate disappointing people.'

'Then don't. Say yes – unless he's not your type, of course.'

'He's good-looking I suppose, but . . .' Briony struggled for words. 'I can't face all that dating stuff right now. I'm not getting involved with anyone again until I'm certain that it's worth it.'

Katie laughed.

'You're starting to sound like Max!'

'Max and I are alike in lots of ways – not that he's noticed.'

'You should give Dave a go. He's a sweet, considerate guy.'

'Then how come you turned him down?'

'I wasn't interested.'

'Why not?'

Katie shrugged. 'Oh, you know.'

Briony nodded like she understood; Katie wished that she understood herself, because she didn't have a clue why she'd been so hard on Dave.

Mr Lucas tore into lesson six with all guns blazing.

'Right! Beauty – what have you got for me?'

When Pete Hazlitt came out with 'Beauty is only skin deep,' Mr Lucas said, 'That tells us more about people than beauty. It means that someone who looks beautiful isn't necessarily a pleasant person.'

Max put up his hand.

'Doesn't it also mean that we put too much value on outward appearance?'

'Good!' said Mr Lucas, beaming. 'You're thinking. Keep it up! And . . . you?' He pointed at Katie.

'Beauty is in the eye of the beholder.'

'Which is another way of saying?'

'That everyone has their own idea of what's beautiful. It's a matter of personal taste.'

'Up to a point. How many of you know the line, *A thing of beauty is a joy forever*?'

Decent show of hands.

'It's a well-known quotation,' said Mr Lucas. 'In fact, it's become so well-known that most people don't think about it any more, but you're going to.'

And all at once it was like a History lesson, because Mr Lucas stuck a transparency of Tutankhamun's death-mask on the overhead projector. 'How many of you would call that beautiful?'

Most people raised their hands.

Mr Lucas went into overdrive, talking about everything that had changed since King Tut's time, but meanwhile the idea of beauty had stayed the same. Beauty had outlasted wars, religious beliefs and natural disasters.

'And can we come to some kind of conclusion?'

Max put up his hand again.

'An object is judged beautiful when it conforms to a set of generally held, but unwritten, aesthetic ideals.'

There was a general, 'Huh?'

'Translate, please,' said Mr Lucas.

'You recognise beauty when you see it, but you can't always define what it is.'

'Excellent! Tomorrow we're going to read

some famous love poems, and we'll come across ideas about beauty in them.'

'And sorrow,' Max said quietly.

And it was freaky, because Katie had been thinking exactly the same thing.

On the way home, for no apparent reason, Max said, 'I'm going to do it!'

'What?'

'Ring her up and talk to her.'

'Way to go!'

'Maybe ask for a date.'

'One step at a time, Max,' Katie said tactfully.

'No. If I leave it too long, someone else is bound to step in.'

'It could be too soon, Max. She just ended a long-term relationship. You don't want to get caught in a rebound situation.'

'Don't I? At least I'd *be* in a situation.'

A car went past. Mr Lucas was driving and Briony was in the passenger seat. Briony waved: Katie waved back; Max didn't.

'Wait for the dust to settle,' said Katie. 'Want me to sound her out for you some time next week?'

'No, I have to do this face-to-face – well, phone-to-phone.'

Katie didn't want to put a damper on Max's new-found assertiveness, but she thought he was on to a loser. Jasmine had always made it clear that she liked Max, but not in the way that he hoped she liked him.

'Up to you. I'll be there for you when you need a shoulder.'

'Thanks, Katie, but I don't think I'll be doing any crying. I've got a good feeling about this.'

Katie didn't have a good feeling; she saw heartache on the horizon, and Max was headed straight for it.

9

Katie got in, fed Cleo, went upstairs intending to do her homework and sat at her table, frowning into space instead. Something was missing – something important that she'd forgotten to do. She ran the day through in her mind to see if she could remember what it was: not a school-thing, not a home-thing, not a Max-thing . . . SHAZAM! Playing Cupid with Briony and Dave hadn't worked out, but Dave didn't know. If Katie didn't warn him asap, Dave could find himself in an embarrassing-rejection scenario.

Down in the hall, Katie hit the phone book and punched-in the number, praying that there was only one Michaels family living in Horn-beam Drive.

A woman answered.

Katie said, 'Is Dave there, please?'

'Yes. Who's calling?'

'Katie Drew.'

'Katie? Not *the* Katie?'

'Er, no, just *a* Katie.'

'I'll fetch him for you.'

It took a few seconds, just enough time for Katie to choose between going round the houses or in Dave's face.

The phone rattled as Dave picked it up.

'Hi, Katie! How you doing?'

'Good. Don't ask her.'

'Who?'

'Briony Lucas.'

'Don't ask her what?'

'To go out with you. She'll say no.'

'Will she?'

'I was talking to her at lunch-time. She's not over her last boyfriend yet. I thought you ought to know.'

Dave sighed.

'Thanks, Katie. Never mind, I'll have to go by myself.'

'Go where?'

'To see that new movie – the one where Shakespeare gets sucked into a time-warp and ends up as a high-school principal?'

'*Bard Timing*?'

'Yeah. Bummer. I hate watching movies on my own.'

'What about your mates?'

'They're action-movie freaks. They're going to *Crucial Jeopardy Three*.'

'Problem sorted!' said Katie. 'Max and I are planning to see *Bard Timing* on Saturday night. Why don't you tag along?'

'I'd be in the way.'

'No you wouldn't. It's not like Max and I are an item.'

'Are you sure Max wouldn't mind?'

'Positive.'

'Can I think about it?'

'Be my guest.'

'OK, I've thought about it. I'd like to, yeah. Thanks for taking pity on me.'

'I'm not. Meet us on the bridge in the Wallgate Centre around seven.'

'Great!'

This was the point where Katie should have said goodbye and rung off, but she didn't and neither did Dave. They hung on until the silence stretched out into awkwardness.

Katie said, 'Was that your mum I was talking to just now?'

'Yes.'

'When I told her my name, she asked me if I was *the* Katie. What did she mean?'

'Um, at Easter, after you ... you know? I guess I talked to her about you. I was pretty down at the time.'

'Sorry.'

'Don't be. It's fine. We're friends now, right?'

'Right.'

'I could use a friend just at the moment,' said Dave, sounding wistful.

'How come?'

'Complications.'

'Such as?'

Dave's voice hardened.

'Well, thanks for calling, Katie. I'll see you on Saturday.'

'Parent in room?'

'You've got it. Bye now.'

Katie put down the phone and thought. So, Dave had a secret? Not only was he Mr Make-over, he was also Man of Mystery; that upgraded him from interesting to intriguing.

Mum staggered into the lounge, clutching the mail from the hall table. She dropped herself into an armchair, kicked off her shoes and wiggled her toes.

'You're late!' Katie said.

'There was a traffic-light failure in town. Chaos!'

'I got a lasagne out of the freezer. It's defrosting in the microwave.'

'My daughter, the angel! How was today?'

'Peculiar.'

'Why?'

'You don't want to know.'

'Of course I do!'

'OK. Jasmine and Jordan broke up, so now Max wants to put the moves on Jasmine, which is a total no-no, but when I told him, he wouldn't listen to me. Plus, Dave has got the hots for Briony, but she doesn't want to know because she's still got a thing for her ex. So it looks like I'll be going to the movies on Saturday with Dave and Max, when they'd both rather be with someone else.'

'You were right,' said Mum. 'I don't want to know.'

'Was your adolescence like this?'

'Like what?'

'Messy.'

'I can't remember. I'm still in denial.'

The microwave pinged; Katie stood up to see to it.

Mum was flicking through the mail, murmuring, 'Bill, bill, bill.' Then she stopped and said, 'Oh!' so sharply that it made Katie pause in the doorway. Mum was gazing at an envelope like it had sprouted fangs and was about to bite her. Her eyes were wide and her face was pink.

'What is it?' Katie asked.

'Hmm?'

'You're blushing.'

'Am I?'

Mum wasn't just blushing, she was rattled.

'Aren't you going to open it?'

'What?'

'The letter.'

'No, I'll save it for later. It's only another bill.'

Katie knew this was a lie, because the envelope didn't have a transparent window.

10

Wednesday had been peculiar, but Thursday was *seriously* peculiar.

It started normally enough. Katie got up, went into the bathroom and showered, dressed for school and was downstairs in time to say goodbye to Mum. After Mum left for work, Katie downed a bowl of cereal and a mug of tea, loaded the dishes into the dishwasher, topped-up Cleo's crunchies, went outside and found Max at the front gate.

'Max – what are you doing here?'

Max looked around, as though to make sure that Katie wasn't talking to someone else.

'Er, waiting for you?'

'But we don't do this! I always call for you.'

'Well this morning is different. Satan tempted me into a change of routine.'

'Ah, funny you should mention a change of routine. You know we're going to *Bard Timing* on Saturday? Guess who wants to come with us!'

Katie gave Max an in-depth, close-up, slow-motion replay of her phone conversation with Dave, and concluded, 'So is that OK with you?'

'I might not be there,' said Max.

'I knew you wouldn't mind. I told Dave so,

but he— Did you just say you might not be there?'

'I may have other plans.'

'That makes things awkward!' Katie said. 'I mean, the three of us together is one thing, but if Dave and I are in a one-to-one, people might think— What other plans?'

'You're not the only one who made a phone call last night.'

Katie could have kicked herself. She'd been so excited about Dave that she'd completely forgotten Max and Jasmine.

'So-rry! Here I am, wittering on, while you're . . . So how did it go?'

'Negotiations are at a delicate stage.'

'She said yes?'

'She said she'd think about it and let me know today.'

'Why don't you take her to *Bard Timing*? We could be a foursome.'

'I'll wait for her to say yes before I make any definite plans. Besides, no offence, Katie, but first dates are crucial. I don't think taking my best mate along is such a good idea. It would look like I needed a minder.'

'Point taken. No sweat, I can ring Dave and cancel.'

'Why would you do that?'

'Because if just the two of us go to the movies, it's like a date.'

'And?'

'It's not like that, Max. Dave and I are friends.'

'Oh really?'

'Yes, really. He won't want to come if you're not there.'

Max shook his head as if he had water in his ears.

'Hang on, I don't get this! Dave's your friend, right?'

'Right.'

'And you're his friend?'

'Right.'

'Then what d'you need me for? If you and he are such big buddies, what's the problem with catching a movie together?'

'Dave might change his mind once he knows that—'

'Don't tell him.'

'Huh?'

'Meet up with him on Saturday and tell him I had to pull out at the last minute.'

Katie wasn't comfortable with the idea, because it would seem too much like a set-up.

'Anyway, this is all hypothetical,' said Max. 'We won't know how we're fixed until I get my answer. Let's not count our chickens.'

Katie wasn't counting anything, she was too busy analysing her feelings. The prospect of not seeing Dave on Saturday night was alarmingly disappointing; and the prospect of having him to herself was so appealing that Katie didn't care to dwell on it for too long. Everything depended on Jasmine.

'I hope she says yes,' Katie muttered, thinking aloud.

'Thanks,' said Max. 'I appreciate the support.'

He wasn't being sarcastic, which made Katie feel guilty. Max was trying to get to first base with the girl of his dreams, Katie was supposed to be his closest friend, and all she could do was think about herself.

Maybe she could do something to help Max out, make his life a little easier.

Since Jasmine was also in the top set, Katie had a chance to observe how she and Max reacted to each other. They stuck firmly to the *when in school, play it cool* rule, and did it so well that they deserved a BAFTA award: no body language, no secret glances; nobody would have twigged that anything was going on. Katie wouldn't have twigged herself if she hadn't known.

Timing was crucial. As soon as the bell rang for the start of lunch break, Katie turned to Briony and Max and said, 'You guys go on to the cafeteria. I'll meet you in a couple of minutes.'

'What?' said Max, looking like Briony was the last person he wanted to be left alone with; Briony didn't seem too chuffed either.

'Must dash!' said Katie, dashing. She made

it to the corridor just as Jasmine went into the girls' loos. Katie followed her, thinking, 'Low-key, subtle, nonchalant!'

When Jasmine stepped out of the cubicle, Katie was standing at one of the washbasins, staring into a mirror as she brushed her hair. Jasmine stood at the neighbouring basin and washed her hands. No one else was around.

Katie said, 'I hear someone made you an offer you might refuse.'

Jasmine boggled.

'How did you find out?'

'You know how it is in this place. Secrets don't stay secret for long.'

'But he only asked me last night!'

'And you told him you'd think about it, yeah?'

Jasmine nodded.

'Are you going to say yes, or what?' Katie demanded.

Jasmine smiled, kind of shy and pleased at the same time.

'It was a shock. I mean, I guessed that he was keen on me, but I didn't think he'd ever do anything about it. When he came out with it, it made me think. He hasn't been a friend, exactly, but I've always felt there was something between us. I never thought about getting together with him before.'

'But you are now?'

'I'm considering it.'

'Considering it yes, or considering it no?'

'Considering it yes. People will talk if I do, but—'

'Who gives a stuff what people say?'

Jasmine's smile contracted.

'You're not going to tell him, are you?'

'And spoil the surprise? No chance!'

'Was he the one who told you?'

'We were talking and it sort of slipped out in passing.'

'I didn't know that you and he were—'

'What?'

'That you talked about stuff like that.'

'We do when it matters, and as far as he's concerned, you matter.'

Jasmine's eyes misted over.

'He's sweet, isn't he?'

Not a term that Katie would ever have applied to Max, but she let it ride.

'He has his good points.'

'I'm nervous,' Jasmine confessed. 'Is that a good sign?'

'You'll be fine. He's nervous too.'

'Is he? That's so—'

'Sweet?'

'Yes. We both feel the same.'

Katie was relieved: Max was in; the way Jasmine was talking, she was going to have to put lead weights in her shoes to keep her feet on the ground. It was weird, because less than a week ago Jasmine had been sorry that Max was crazy about her, now she'd done a complete about-face.

Maybe that was how people acted when they were in love.

Max showed uncharacteristic restraint, but he finally let go at the end of the day, as he and Katie were walking down Church Lane. He punched the air and said, 'Yess!'

'Got a result?'

'The young lady in question responded affirmatively.'

Katie was pleased, but puzzled.

'When was this?'

'Lunch-time.'

'But you were with Briony and me at lunch-time. I didn't see—'

'It happened when you weren't there.'

'I know it happened when I wasn't there, otherwise I would've been there when it happened! How did you manage to—?'

'I asked her again, she opened her mouth and *yes* came out.'

'When's the big day?'

'Saturday.'

'What's the venue?'

'Meet at Manconi's, then go to that new tapas bar.'

'Isn't that a bit pricey?'

'Expense is no object.'

'Wouldn't you be better off at the movies? It'll give you both something to talk about.'

'We have plenty to talk about,' Max said. 'I've got a lot of catching-up to do.'

So, Max was happy and Jasmine was happy – which left Katie with the problem of Dave. To come clean or not to come clean? If she did, she might lose out; if she didn't, she'd be dishonest. Everything was supposed to be fair in love and war, but . . .

Katie was so confused that later on, she asked Mum about it.

'Mum, suppose you asked somebody out, like not asking-them-out asking them out, just asking them out, but deep down you really *were* asking them out, would you go out with them without letting them know first?'

'Go for it,' Mum said.

Katie jerked in shock.

'Huh?'

'Go for it,' Mum repeated.

Katie laughed.

'What's funny?' said Mum.

'That's pretty good advice, coming from you!'

Mum gave Katie one of her Mona Lisa smiles and said, 'Don't do as I do, do as I tell you.'

'Meaning?'

'Meaning that's my final word. If you say anything more, I'll turn into a neurotic mother and ask you for names and addresses.'

Katie knew when she ought to shut up, and did.

11

Friday was OK, but didn't go entirely smoothly, for which Katie was grateful. Smooth made her paranoid, because it was generally a sign that the sky was ready to come crashing down.

When she called for Max on the way to school, he was still getting ready, so his mum invited Katie in to wait.

Mrs Fielding was fond of Katie – both her children were male, and in some ways she treated Katie as the daughter she'd never had – but this morning there was a glint of anxiety behind the welcome in her eyes.

'Katie,' she said quietly, 'is something wrong with Max?'

'Not that I know of – why?'

'He was acting strangely last night.'

'Oh?'

'He was cheerful. He chatted to me, helped me to get dinner ready, and then when his father came home, Max spoke to him. It was odd, not like Max at all.'

'He was in a pretty good mood after school.'

'Yes,' said Mrs Fielding, 'I noticed that. He was, well, almost happy. He hasn't been dabbling with drink or drugs, has he?'

'Absolutely not!'

'I couldn't help wondering. It was the only explanation I could think of that would account for it. Is it likely to last long?'

'Hard to say.'

Mrs Fielding chewed her bottom lip.

'After raising two sons, and sending one off to university, you'd expect me to know all there was to know about teenage boys, wouldn't you? But when something like this happens, you're right back to square one. It's not because of anything I've done, is it – or his father?'

'No. I'd tell you if it was.'

'That's something, anyway.' Mrs Fielding looked on the bright side. 'Perhaps it's just a passing phase, and in a few days he'll be morose again, and everything can get back to normal.'

'Normal?' said Katie. 'I don't want to bring you down, Mrs Fielding, but remember, Max may be your son and my mate, but he's still a bloke.'

'True! Men are so fickle and unpredictable, aren't they? A complete mystery. Thank you, Katie. You've taken a weight off my mind.'

Max clumped down the stairs and appeared in the kitchen doorway. He grinned at Katie.

'All set?'

'Yup.'

Max pecked his mum on the cheek.

'Farewell, Mother dear. I hope you have a satisfying and fulfilling day.'

Max didn't catch Mrs Fielding's little shudder, but Katie did. She waited until she and Max were out on the street, then said, 'Cool it, Max! Your mum's getting concerned.'

'About what?'

'You. She thinks you're happy.'

'I *am* happy. What's wrong with being happy?'

'It's freaking-out your parents. Show some consideration and play it down, will you? They're having trouble coping with Mr Sunshine.'

'Hmm!' Max said thoughtfully. 'Maybe I have overdone things a bit. I asked Dad a question about that Maths homework last night and he was—' Max pulled a terrified face. 'I shouldn't startle him like that, it's bad for his blood pressure.'

'And quit smiling! If some Year Eleven thug catches you smiling like that, he'll think you're smiling at him and you'll get your head kicked in.'

Despite Katie's warning, Max continued on a high. He even included Briony in the conversation at lunch-time, and cracked a few gags that made her laugh. He gave Jasmine a wide berth though, and she did the same. Katie admired their ability to maintain the indifference act; Max obviously had more willpower than she'd given him credit for.

Friday's major blip occurred at the end of the school day. Max and Briony spent the afternoon in a double Art lesson, while Katie had double Drama. As she was walking down from the Drama Suite, Katie met Dave coming the other way. Her pulse rocketed, her knees wobbled and her brain scrambled.

'Hi, Katie!'

'Dave! Um, er, hi!'

'Are we still on for tomorrow night?'

'I guess.'

'Good! I'm looking forward to it.'

'Um, me too!'

A red neon sign in Katie's head flashed up: GUILT! GUILT! GUILT!

'Actually, Dave, about tomorrow?'

'Yes?'

'Would you mind if . . .? Would it be a drag if . . .?'

Dave looked crestfallen.

'Are you trying to tell me that you want to pull out, Katie?'

'Not at all! It's just, you see—'

'Because if you do, don't pussyfoot around, just say it.'

'I'm not going to say it! I don't want to pull out.'

Dave relaxed.

'I'm glad. Should I dress formally – DJ, black bow tie?'

'No, just wear what you'd usually—' Katie

saw Dave's joke too late and closed her mouth before she made an even bigger idiot of herself.

'You feeling all right, Katie?'

'Me? Fine!'

'You seem a little—'

'I just had Drama,' Katie said quickly. 'It was intense. I'm kind of still in character, you know? Sometimes I get so into it that it's difficult to switch off. I had to play this girl who's lost control of herself – like she says what she's really thinking instead of keeping it back and being polite?'

'Yeah! It would be a strange world if people did that, wouldn't it?'

'Oh, I don't know. Like if I'd said, *Dave, you're looking great!* instead of, *Hi,* would that have been strange?'

'Only if it was what you were really thinking, and not if I'd already said that *you* were looking great because it was what *I* was really thinking. Then you'd just be returning the compliment.'

'But I'd have to mean it, if it was what I really thought.'

Dave was uneasy.

'Are we still talking about acting here?'

'Certainly we are! I'd never come out with something like that. Not that I wouldn't think – it would be too – I'd be . . .'

There wasn't an end to the sentence, because Katie didn't have a clue what she'd be.

'You'd be the part you were acting instead of you,' said Dave. 'I like the real you better.'

Katie's hopes rose and collapsed like a failed soufflé. Dave wasn't talking about the real her, he was talking about what he *thought* was the real her.

12

Katie was up first on Saturday. After feeding Cleo she made herself toast and tea, and went to watch cartoons on kids' TV.

Mum got up half an hour later, came into the lounge, glanced at the TV and said, 'What's this? You're too young to be nostalgic!'

'I'm practising for when I'm older,' Katie said. 'Anyhow, it's not nostalgia, it's self-indulgence. I finished all my homework last night, so I can afford to be mindless and enjoy that Saturday-morning feeling.'

'What have you got planned for today?'

Katie's defences went on to red alert. She didn't want Mum to know about Dave, because Mum wouldn't understand about its being a non-date date.

'Not a lot. Supermarket with you, then tonight I'm going to a movie.'

'With Max?'

Katie had the distinct impression that Mum was prying, and sidestepped the truth by saying, 'Yeah, Max will be around.'

'What time will you be back?'

'You know what time I'll be back. My curfew is ten-thirty, remember?'

'Make it eleven,' Mum said.

'Huh?'

'I'm giving you an extension to celebrate your new status as a GCSE student. And there's no need to come to the supermarket. I've made an appointment at the hairdresser's this morning. I'll do the shopping afterwards.'

'A hairdo? What's the occasion?'

'Your nagging finally wore me down. I'm going for a restyle.'

'Not short and spiky?' Katie said apprehensively.

'Nothing so radical, but it's time for a change. I've worn my hair like this for years.'

Ever since Dad died, to be precise; Katie counted this as progress.

'White and orange streaks are trendy.'

'I don't want to be trendy. I'd look like mutton dressed as lamb. I'm no Spring chicken, you know.'

'You don't get mutton from chickens.'

'You know what I mean.'

'You don't want to be one of those sad old tarts who try to look younger than they are?'

'Exactly.'

'Thirty-eight isn't old.'

Katie waited for Mum to make some comment about being past it, the way she always did, but instead Mum said, 'No, it isn't, is it?'

There was a sparkle in Mum's eyes; Katie wondered what had put it there.

'Did you have a good day at work yesterday?'

'Not particularly – why?'

'You're chirpy this morning.'

'Is that a problem? Would you prefer me to be cranky?'

'No, chirpy is fine!'

'I'm so glad that you approve.'

Katie let it drop, not wanting to spoil the moment.

Mum returned from shopping with a bootload of supermarket bags and a jaw-length bob that suited the lines of her face.

'You look terrific!' said Katie.

'You don't think it's—?'

'Definitely not.'

'It's not too—?'

'It's perfect. Whoever you're trying to impress is going to be impressed.'

'I did it to please myself.'

'Then be pleased.'

Mum wasn't entirely convinced.

'Of course, I can always grow it out if I decide it's not me.'

'Give yourself a break will you, Mum? It's *very* you. I can't remember the last time you looked so you.'

Mum smiled and said, 'Would you give me a hand unloading the car, please?'

It wasn't until much, much later that Katie twigged this was the point at which Mum changed the subject.

Even though she did her best not to be early, at 6:45 Katie was standing on the bridge over the river that divided the Wallgate Shopping Centre in two. The centre was less than a year old and Katie wasn't used to it yet, but she'd already forgotten what had been on the site before the centre was built, which was alarming. Wallgate was basically a gigantic shopping mall with a multi-screen cinema and a multi-storey car park attached. You could eat and drink your way around the world in the restaurants and bars that lined the banks of the river.

The sun hadn't set so the sky was still light, but the shadows were spreading at ground level. Katie gazed at the twisting reflections in the water and wondered how she was going to explain Max's absence to Dave. A tight knot of anticipation in her stomach gave her an insight into how Cleo must feel when she had a furball.

'This is not a date,' Katie kept reminding herself. 'No pressure, no reason to get stressed. This is two friends going to a movie. It's irrelevant that I'm a girl and he's a drop-dead hunk. We're going to enjoy each other's company and there'll be no more to it than that, unfortunately. No! Delete *unfortunately*!'

At seven o'clock Katie looked around, expecting Dave to appear any second; at 7:10 she wished that he would; at 7:20 she doubted it, and by 7:35 she was convinced that he wasn't going to.

Since it wasn't technically a date, Dave hadn't *actually* stood her up, but it sure felt as if he had. He must have changed his mind, or received a more attractive offer, or maybe he was getting his own back for how she'd treated him at Easter.

Katie's stomach unknotted itself. What to do now? *Bard Timing* was due to start in five minutes, and if she ran flat-out she might make it, but she wasn't in the mood for sprinting or movies. She wouldn't be able to concentrate on the plot because she'd spend the whole time fretting about Dave. Might as well chuck her money into the river and waste it that way. Going home would mean a grilling from Mum and a long, humiliating explanation – just what Katie didn't need.

She began to devise the most complicated and time-consuming return journey that she could think of: a stroll to the station, catch a train to Whitwood – say forty-five minutes – then wait for a bus. That should have her home about—

'Katie!'

She wheeled around and saw Dave running past Debenhams, swerving to avoid passers-by, his pale overcoat flapping like wings. He ran on to the bridge and stood panting in front of Katie.

'Sorry – bus got stuck – there was a tailback – traffic-light failure!'

'I thought you'd forgotten.'

'As if! Have we missed the beginning of the movie?'

'Yes.'

'Sorry! Did Max go on ahead?'

'No, and I'm the one who should be saying sorry. Max is on a date. I knew he wasn't coming yesterday and I meant to tell you when I met you outside the Drama Suite, but I didn't because I didn't think you'd want to go to the movies if it was just you and me, and now you probably don't even want to be here because you think I arranged this on purpose, which would make me a totally dishonest person and put you right off me. So you can tell me to get lost if you like, because that's what I deserve and I apologise for spoiling your evening.'

'You haven't.'

'I know! I wasn't thinking straight and – huh?'

'You haven't spoiled my evening. Not yet.'

'Really?'

'To be honest with you, I'm relieved that it's just the two of us.'

'Why?'

'It gives us a chance to talk.'

'About?'

'Whatever you'd like to talk about. You mind not seeing the movie?'

'No.'

'Nor do I. Let's walk.'

High Street was strange: there was hardly anyone around; most of the shops were still lit, mannequins posed and *special offer* signs glared in the windows, but there were no customers for them to persuade. The bouncers outside the Irish pub looked sleepy-eyed and bored.

Dave and Katie talked school, teachers and people they had in common; they compared tastes in music and TV programmes. Dave wasn't who Katie thought he was. He'd been the nerd who fancied her, then he'd turned into Mr Tasty, but neither of the boxes fitted him. He had a dry sense of humour that was easy to miss, and he seemed to have done a lot more growing up since Year Nine than the guys he hung-out with.

They wound up on a bench outside the Municipal Museum, relaxing as they grew used to each other. Katie had to struggle not to stare at Dave, but then they established an eye-contact that continued after the conversation petered out. When they noticed the silence they laughed nervously and looked away, pretending that the eye-contact hadn't happened.

'Hey!' said Katie. 'When I rang you the other day, you said something about needing a friend. What was that about?'

'Caitlin,' said Dave. His voice sounded like a closing door.

'Who's Caitlin?'

'A girl I met in Corfu. She was the one who talked me into the hair-job.'

'She was right.'

'Yeah. Caitlin was right about a lot of things.'

Katie picked up on Dave's air of regret and said, 'Holiday romance?'

'It wasn't supposed to be. We were supposed to have fun with no ties, but . . .'

'You got involved.'

'I did, only I didn't find out until I was on the plane home.'

'Where does she live?'

'Manchester.'

'Ouch! Long way away.'

'Just as well. There's no danger of running into her.'

'You miss her?'

Dave had trouble answering, like he hadn't considered it before.

'I'm not sure. I miss who I was when we were together. She made me feel like someone.' Dave let out a breath and shook his head. 'This is going to sound crazy, but you're the only person I've talked to about Caitlin. My parents are – well, *parents* – and my mates are . . . you know, not oversubscribed in the sensitivity department.'

A dumb question that had been rattling around Katie's mind slipped past the guards and escaped into her mouth.

'Was she pretty?'

'She looked a lot like you. That's what first

made me—' Dave swallowed hard. 'I'm starving! Are you hungry? Fancy a burger? My shout.'

'No it's not. I'll pay for my own.'

'Tell you what, I'll buy yours if you'll buy mine.'

'Fair enough!'

On the way to the burger bar, Katie noticed a couple snogging in a doorway not far from the tapas place. She thought she recognised Jasmine and whispered, 'Way to go, Max!'

Then the couple broke from their clinch, and Katie saw that she was wrong. It was Jasmine all right, but the boy she'd been snogging was Gavin Macey.

Something weird was going on.

Katie was in by 10:50, feeling a bit head-in-the-clouds because the evening with Dave had been the *best*. Just before they parted, Dave said, 'We must do this again,' and Katie said, 'Yes,' and they'd left it there. She hadn't wanted to be pushy, but took Dave's interest in seeing her again as a plus.

Mum was watching TV.

'Have a good time?' she asked Katie.

'Yeah. You?'

'Likewise.'

Katie sat down, looked at the screen and saw Dave's eyes, heard his laugh.

'How was the movie?' said Mum.

'We didn't go in the end. We just took a walk and talked.'

'Yes,' Mum said dreamily. 'Talking can be nice, can't it?'

Katie peered at her mother.

'You're wearing eye shadow.'

'Yes. I bought it after I'd been to the hairdresser this morning.'

'And that's a new lipstick, isn't it?'

'Yes.'

'You got all dolled up to sit at home on your own?'

'Must be the Change of Life,' said Mum. 'Some women get it early.'

Katie didn't believe a word of it.

Something *radically* weird was going on.

13

Right after breakfast next morning, Mum took the car for its weekly treat at the car-wash, and Katie got on the phone to Max.

'What went wrong last night?' she asked him.

'Thanks for the vote of confidence, Katie! I hate to disappoint you, but nothing went wrong.'

'Max, this is sad! Drop the act. I know.'

'Know what?'

'That it didn't work out. I saw Jasmine last night. She was with Gavin Macey.'

There was a longish pause, then Max said, 'What's Jasmine got to do with anything?'

'You and she were— I mean, I talked to her on Thursday and she said—' But now she came to think about it, Katie couldn't recall Jasmine's mentioning Max's name, and he hadn't mentioned hers either. 'Max, who were you with last night?'

'Briony – who else?'

'Briony? Are you telling me that you and Briony – she and you—?'

'That's right.'

'You rat, Max! How could you let me go on thinking that you were taking Jasmine out?'

'I didn't. You did it to yourself. How could

I know what you were thinking, Katie? I'm not telepathic. How did it go with Dave?'

'I think he wants to go out with me again.'

'And do you?'

'I think so.'

'Do yourself a favour, Katie – think less and know more. Sometimes going with your feelings is the right thing to do.'

Katie held the phone at arm's length so she could gawk at it. The voice on the line sounded like Max's, but it wasn't saying the kind of things that Max said. Where was the doomed pessimist she'd come to know and love?

Katie brought the phone back to her ear and said, 'Max, have you been reading one of those ditzy little self-help books that are supposed to keep you calm?'

'No, I've been talking to Briony. She made me feel . . . sort of . . .'

'Someone?'

'Yes! How did you know?'

'A friend told me,' Katie said.

When she hung up the receiver, Katie rewound her memory tapes and fast-forwarded, freeze-framed them until they started to make sense. What she'd taken to be Max's dislike of Briony was actually shyness. Briony made Max quiet, like Dave made Katie run off at the mouth.

Katie pictured Max and Briony together, but they changed into herself and Dave: walking hand in hand, dancing at The Red Airplane, hugging at a bus stop . . .

'Oh, no!' Katie wailed. 'I'm a closet romantic!'

It was the toughest thing she'd ever had to admit to herself.

Mum was way later coming back from the car-wash than she should have been. Katie was just getting to the point of thinking that there must have been some kind of accident, when she heard the car pull up in the drive. She went into the hall and stood with her hands on her hips, waiting for Mum to open the front door.

'Where have you *been*?'

'At the car-wash,' Mum said.

'For two hours?'

'I went to the one on Shepherd's Mount. There was a queue. Then, as I was driving home, I remembered I had to make some phone calls, so I pulled in and used my mobile.'

'And you didn't think to ring and let me know? It didn't occur to you that I might be worried?'

'You get chatting and time flies by,' Mum said with a shrug.

'Well next time, I'd appreciate it if you called to let me know what you're doing. I nearly rang the police!'

'You know what this sounds like?'

'What?'

'It sounds like you're the mother and I'm the teenager. Nag, nag, nag!'

'Cut it out, Mum!'

'When are you going to understand that I'm not a kid any more? I have my own life to live!'

'Mu-um!'

'You keep telling me to act responsibly, but when it comes down to it, you just don't trust me, do you?'

'That's it!' Katie snapped. 'There's no talking to you when you're in this mood. I'm going to get lunch ready.'

Mum's freakiness continued through lunch and on into the afternoon. Finally, Katie couldn't stand it any more.

'I'm going for a walk!' she announced.

'Want company?'

'No!'

'Touchy, touchy! Can't take being wound up, huh?'

'I can't take you getting off on it. See you later.'

'Whenever,' Mum said.

Katie stomped out of the house, wondering whether she was the one who'd lost the plot, or the rest of the world had. She was at screaming point; if anything else unexpected happened, she'd be tipped right over the edge.

Something unexpected happened: Briony turned the corner at the end of the street, faltered when she caught sight of Katie, recovered her poise and walked towards her, smiling sheepishly.

'Fancy meeting you,' Katie said.

'I had to get away from my dad,' said Briony. 'He's driving me round the bend! He's acting ultra-hearty, like making jokes and being considerate? He's up to something.'

'Must be the time of year. My mum's acting peculiarly too. Could they be having a mid-life crisis?'

'Who knows?' Briony sighed. 'I meant to come over anyway. I tried to ring you this morning, but Dad was hogging the phone, and then it was lunch, so I took a chance that you'd be in.'

'Funny, I was going to phone you. That was some sneaky stunt you and Max pulled on me last night.'

'We weren't sneaky! He told me you knew about it.'

'Crossed wire – but don't get your lingerie in a loop. I'm cool with it.'

'I was afraid you might not be. I know how important you are to Max. I didn't want to come between you.'

'Don't flatter yourself, Bri. Max and I go back a long way. I warn you though, hurt his feelings and I'll be on your case.'

'D'you think he's serious about me? He didn't go out with me because he couldn't go out with Jasmine, did he?'

'When I rang him this morning, he didn't

give me the impression that you're the consolation prize.'

'There's just one problem about all this,' Katie said with a sigh.

'Oh?'

'My dad.'

'Because he's Max's English teacher?'

'Because he's Dad. If he finds out, he'll invite Max over and lecture him.'

'Max will handle it. It'll take more than a parental lecture to put the frighteners on him.'

'The trouble with Dad is, he's only got me to think about. If he had a social life of his own, he might ease up a bit.'

'No girlfriend?'

Briony laughed.

'Are you kidding? No one measures up to Mum. He's built her up into this ideal woman because he only remembers the good bits. He used to hit the bottle and get sentimental about her – you know, look at her photo and cry? He hasn't done that in over a year, but he won't try and find somebody else. He says that once you're over forty it's too much hassle.'

'My mum's the same. Grown-ups! The older they get, the bigger the headache they give you.'

'Ain't that the truth! Except the ache Dad gives me is lower down.'

A cold wind made Katie thrust her hands deeper into the pockets of her jacket; Briony shivered.

'Want to come back to my place?' said Katie. 'We can slag off our parents in comfort – plus I do a mean hot chocolate.'

'With marshmallow melts?'

'Is there any other kind?'

When Mum heard the front door open, she called out, 'Katie? You weren't long.'

'I bumped into a friend,' said Katie. She eased Briony into the doorway of the lounge and stood beside her. 'This is Briony.'

Mum's eyebrows shot up.

'Briony?'

'Briony Lucas. She's Mr Lucas's daughter.'

'Mr Lucas?'

'My new English teacher. I told you about him.'

Mum jumped to her feet as though she'd been stung.

'Of course! How stupid of me! Hello, Briony.'

'Hello, Mrs Drew,' Briony said.

'Please come in. Do sit down. Would you like something?'

'Katie was going to make me a hot chocolate.'

'Good idea! I think I'll join you.' Mum looked at Katie. 'That's three hot chocolates, Katie, and bring a plate of biscuits as well.'

Katie was miffed.

'What did your last slave die of?'

'Insolence,' said Mum. 'Now, tell me, Briony . . .'

And for the next hour it was: how are you settling in, what's the school like, have you made many friends, does your father like his new job?

Katie couldn't get a word in.

Eventually, Mum exhausted her supply of questions. Briony said that she had to be going, and Katie went to the door with her.

'Sorry about that, Bri. Mum's not usually that nosy. She's going through kind of a funny patch at the moment.'

Briony's eyes were radiant.

'Your mum's brilliant! She's it!'

'What?'

'The answer to my problem.'

'What problem?'

'The me-and-Max problem.'

'This is probably just me being thick, but I don't have the faintest idea what you're talking about. See, there are these things called words, and if you put them in the right order, they—.'

'My dad,' said Briony, holding up her left index finger. 'Your mum.' She held up her right index finger, and brought the fingers together so that they formed a cross like the kiss at the end of a letter.

The penny went DING!

'Bri, you're a genius!' Katie gasped.

14

The snag with brilliant ideas, Katie discovered, was putting them into operation. If Mum and Mr Lucas had been teenagers, it would be easy to arrange an 'accidental' meeting at school or in town; if they'd been pensioners, Katie could have set them up at an over-60s club; but being the age they were made things awkward. Katie devoted most of Sunday evening to coming up with something and drew a blank.

Monday morning, on the way to school, she explained everything to Max. Max appeared to approve in principle, but when Katie said, 'What are we going to do about it?' he stopped dead in the middle of the pavement.

'*We?* Count me out, Katie. This is none of my business.'

'Oh yes it is!'

'How come?'

'Because if Mr Lucas shares quality time with Mum, he'll have less time to worry about Briony and he'll stop coming the overprotective parent. That takes heat off you.'

Max lowered one eyebrow and raised the other.

'I don't like it! When it comes to adults, I

adopt the same policy as wildlife documentary-makers – strictly no interference.'

'Don't wimp out on me, Max! We have to pull together here. Don't you want to be part of a beautiful love story?'

'Yes, but I'd prefer it to be *my* beautiful love story.'

Katie adopted her hard-done-by voice.

'I tried to help you with Jasmine, didn't I?'

'I didn't want to be helped with Jasmine!'

'I know, but that's not the point, is it?'

Max growled and started walking again.

Katie said, 'What if Briony and I pretended to disappear? Mr Lucas and Mum would be thrown together, then they'd comfort each other and—'

'Oh, be *real*!' said Max. 'Do you watch too many made-for-TV movies, or what? You have to find something they've got in common and work from there.'

'All they have in common is that I'm Mum's daughter, Mr Lucas is my teacher and I'm friends with his daughter.'

'Hmm, not a lot to go on. Does your mum have any hobbies – golf or tennis?'

'No.'

'Scratch that then. What is she interested in?'

'She reads historical novels and watches the news. She's big on contributing to charity.'

'Which charity?'

'You name it! Save the Children, World

Wildlife Fund, Amnesty, the Cat Protection League—'

'Compassion,' said Max.

'Sorry?'

'Go for her soft underbelly.'

'How?'

'I don't know – she's *your* mum, for crying out loud! You should know how to get round her better than I do. Make her feel sorry for Mr Lucas, like he's a deserving cause who needs her support.'

Katie brooded for a moment, then said, 'How d'you get round your parents?'

'I sulk until I get my own way, and if that doesn't work I throw a tantrum,' Max said.

At break, Katie had a close encounter of the unusual kind with Gavin Macey, who sidled up to her and said, 'Can I have a word, Katie?'

'Sure.'

Gavin eyed Max and Briony.

'It's, er, kind of personal.'

Max and Briony made a tactical withdrawal, but not so far away that Max couldn't eavesdrop.

'I owe you one,' said Gavin.

'Yeah?'

'Jasmine said you talked to her last week, helped her to make up her mind about me. I just wanted to say thanks.'

'No need,' said Katie. 'If I can do something

to make people's lives happier, that's reward enough for me.'

Gavin was moved; it made his eyes go pathetic.

'Cheers, Katie! You're a top girl.'

Gavin went on his way and Katie rejoined Max and Briony.

'Top girl?' said Max. 'Where did you get that line about making people's lives happier – a Miss World contest? You're such a hypocrite, Katie!'

'I am not!' Katie protested. 'Gavin's happy, isn't he? So's Jasmine – and how about what I did for you two?'

'Refresh my memory, what *did* you do for us two?'

'I introduced you. If I hadn't been trust-worthy and level-headed, Mr Davis wouldn't have asked me to look after Briony, and you two wouldn't have met.'

'But we're in the same form,' said Briony. 'We were bound to meet.'

'Yeah,' Katie agreed, 'but it might have taken you ages. Don't bother being grateful, guys. I was only doing what mates do.'

Max pantomimed stumbling.

'Careful with that ego, Katie,' he said. 'I just tripped over it.'

At lunch-time, in the cafeteria, Katie had a non-encounter with Dave.

Max and Briony had it easy: because they

were both friends of Katie's, they could be seen together without provoking comment, but Katie and Dave couldn't. Dave had to sit with his mates on the other side of the room and join in their banter. He couldn't even risk a look in Katie's direction.

'You're staring,' Max warned Katie.

'No I'm not.'

'OK, you're not staring at Dave – you're hoovering him up with your eyes. If you keep up the deep-and-meaningful expression, some-one's going to suss you.'

'What's he doing with those jerks anyhow?'

'Playing pass-the-brain-cell. The others rely on Dave because he's the only one who's got any brain-cells.'

'At least when he talks to me we have an intelligent conversation.'

'How true!' said Max. 'It's clearly your duty to rescue him from his unsavoury friends.'

Briony giggled, stopped and said, 'Sorry, Katie!'

Katie didn't respond to the apology, because Dave stood up to take his tray over to the collection-trolley. She hadn't finished eating, but Katie grabbed her tray and tried not to run as she crossed the cafeteria.

'Oh, hi, Katie!'

'Hi, Dave.'

'How are you?'

'Fine. You?'

'Fine.'

Dave held open the lid of the swing-bin so that Katie could scrape in her leftovers.

'I'll call you at five,' he murmured.

'Check!'

Katie walked back to Max and Briony, thinking, 'WHEEEE!'

The rest of the afternoon was a rose-tinted blur.

Katie did her homework in the lounge, so that she could be nearer the phone. She was prepping for a timed essay on a poem by Lord Byron that began:

She walks in beauty, like the night
Of cloudless climes and starry skies.

Katie thought that she'd cracked it: like love, the night was big and beautiful, but also like love, it was easy to get lost in. Byron was saying there was hope this time, because the night came provided with stars that would help him navigate.

There was a whole section on love in the poetry book that Katie was working from. She browsed through, hoping to pick up a few tips. All the usual suspects had been rounded up – Shakespeare, Wordsworth, Ted Hughes – plus a lot of other poets Katie had never heard of. According to them, love made you delerious or suicidal. Either way, there didn't seem to be a lot of laughter involved, so maybe a GSOH wasn't as vital as Katie had thought. One poem

stood out because it seemed to sum everything
up.

> *I fell for a girl.*
> *I kissed her*
> *And she said she loved me too.*
> *But who I am,*
> *Or who she is,*
> *Or why it happened,*
> *Only the gods can say.*

To Katie's amazement, the poet had lived in
Greece around 100 AD. Not much had
changed since then: love still took people by
surprise and messed with their heads.

Katie thought, 'Ancient Greek, two thou-
sand years old, WLTM female who can explain
why people fall in love.'

Right on cue, the phone rang and Katie
bolted out of her chair to answer it.

'Hello?'

'Hello, Katie. Sorry I didn't ring yesterday.
We went to visit my grandparents in London
and we didn't get back till gone ten.'

'That's all right.'

'I *wanted* to ring you.'

'That's even more all right.'

'I enjoyed myself on Saturday.'

'Me too.'

'A lot.'

'Me too.'

'You know you said yes when I said we

should do it again? Did you mean it, or were you being polite?'

'I meant it. I don't do polite.'

Dave laughed.

'Yeah, I remember! So, the thing is, I rang to ask if you'll go out with me next Saturday, but before you answer I want to get something clear.'

'What?'

'I'm asking for a date. Like a you-and-me-together kind of date. Just us.'

'Yes.'

'Um, was that a yes-you've-made-it-clear, or a yes-I'll-go-on-a-date-with-you?'

'Both.'

'Really?'

'Uh-huh.'

'You're not stringing me along, or saying yes because you feel bad about last Easter?'

'Dave, I *want* to go on a date with you.'

'Honestly?'

'I can hardly wait!'

'Wow!'

'Yeah, that's how I feel.'

'You do?'

'Yes.'

'Wow!' said Dave.

Over dinner, Katie said casually, 'You made a big impression on Briony, Mum. She likes you.'

'The feeling's mutual,' Mum said, equally as casually. 'She's a very pleasant girl.'

'Her mum died five years ago.'

'What a shame!'

'She misses her. It must be rough on Mr Lucas, raising a teenage girl on his own.'

'Tell me about it.'

Katie back-tracked rapidly.

'I didn't mean it wasn't rough on you too, but we can talk about girl-stuff. Briony finds it difficult to do that with her dad.'

'When do you and I ever talk about girl-stuff?'

'Sometimes.'

'Not often!'

'That's because you've done such an excellent job on me. There must be times when Mr Lucas feels he could do with a few tips.'

'If Briony is anything to go by, he's managing more than adequately.'

Dead end; Katie changed direction.

'It can't be easy, moving to a place where you don't know anybody. Big towns can be lonely, can't they?'

Mum put down her knife and fork.

'Katie, where are you going with this?'

'I thought we might invite Briony and Mr Lucas round for a meal some time.'

Mum looked horrified.

'A meal?'

'As a friendly gesture. How about lunch on Sunday?'

'Sunday?'

'Yeah, you know, the day between Saturday and Monday?'

Mum got a grip.

'I understand where you're coming from, Katie, and I'm glad that you're showing consideration towards others, but I think Briony's father should be given more time to make friends of his own before we thrust hospitality on him. Besides, I'll have a lot on this weekend.'

'You will?'

'I'm going out on Saturday evening. One of my colleagues is retiring and I've been invited to his leaving do. I won't be in much before half-eleven and I don't relish the prospect of getting up at the crack of dawn on Sunday to cook lunch for four.'

'Another time then?'

'Perhaps.'

'The weekend after next?'

Mum's shoulders sagged.

'Katie, I've had a hard day and I need to unwind. Would you mind backing off, please? I'll think about it and let you know.'

So much for the soft underbelly approach. Katie was left with no choice – if Mum was going to get together with Mr Lucas, Katie was going to have to be devious.

15

Walking to school next day, Katie said to Max, 'Isn't it amazing how you think and think and think about something, and then one morning you wake up and the answer's right there in your head?'

'It would be, if it had ever happened to me,' Max said.

'I spent hours flogging my buns off, and all the time it was staring me in the face.'

'Congratulations, Katie! I'm pleased for you. What are you on about?'

'Mum and Mr Lucas. I had a go at making her feel sorry for him, but it didn't get me anywhere. This time it's sorted.'

'The darkness is beginning to clear, but I still can't see—'

'It's like you said about finding something they have in common. I did.'

'What is it?'

'Me.'

Katie gave Max the details. When she finished, Max whistled in admiration.

'Blinder!' he said. 'You've really outdone yourself. Just one tiny flaw.'

'What?'

'As soon as they get together, they'll know

it's a set-up and they'll both be after your blood.'

'No they won't! The magic will take over.'

'The magic?'

'Chemistry. Instant attraction. Love at first sight.'

'I don't know how to put it to you gently, Katie, but this is the *real* world. Stuff like that just doesn't happen.'

'Weren't you and Briony instantly attracted?'

'No, it took about ten seconds.'

'There you go!'

'But we're teenagers, Katie! Teenagers are *supposed* to fall in love at first sight. It's different for adults. They're mature, cautious, and it takes them longer to get going.'

'Everybody is a teenager underneath,' Katie said sweepingly. 'Deep down inside we've all got that wild, reckless thing. People don't grow up, they just get older.'

The timed essay on the poem by Byron was conducted under exam conditions – in silence, with Mr Lucas issuing regular time-checks. Katie covered two and a half sides of A4, wrapped it up with a dazzling conclusion, and spent the last few minutes psyching herself up for what she had to do next.

'Pens down!' said Mr Lucas. 'When the bell goes, leave your essays on the tables and please make sure that you've written your name at the top of each sheet.'

The bell rang and the class filed out. Katie hung on, making sure that she was last.

'Mr Lucas, can I talk to you for a minute?'

'Yes, Katie, but don't take too long. I have a date.'

'You do?'

'With a cup of coffee in the staffroom. What seems to be your problem?'

'Oh, there's no problem – I mean, there is, but it's not *my* problem.'

'Then whose is it?'

'My mum's. She's worried about me.'

Mr Lucas smiled.

'That's par for the course, isn't it? Most parents worry about their children.'

'I know, but Mum's worried about my English.'

'She shouldn't be. From what I know of your work so far, I can confidently say that—'

'It's because you're new,' Katie interrupted. 'She's known all my other teachers for years, but she doesn't know you. She's anxious we might not hit it off, because if we didn't, I wouldn't be as motivated as if we did. She's afraid that there might be a personality clash.'

'And is there?'

'No, but that doesn't stop her worrying. I've told her that everything's fine, but . . .' Katie delivered the knock-out punch. 'Not all adults understand young people the way that you do. I wondered . . .'

'What?'

'Could I make an appointment for Mum to have a chat with you – say Friday, after school?'

Mr Lucas tensed slightly.

'Friday?'

'If it's convenient.'

'It's not inconvenient, Katie, but it does strike me as rather unnecessary.'

'Please, Mr Lucas! It would calm Mum down, which would help *me* calm down. Just ten minutes of your time would make an awful lot of difference.'

Mr Lucas was in a corner and there was no way out.

'Very well, Katie. Tell your mother that I'll make myself available in the English department office between three-thirty and four o'clock – and tell her that I'll only be saying good things about you.'

Katie faked a huge sigh of relief.

'Thanks, Mr Lucas!' She made to go, but Mr Lucas stopped her.

'Just a moment, Katie. Since you're here . . . you and Max Fielding are friends, aren't you?'

'Yes.'

'I notice that he and Briony seem to be showing an interest in each other.'

Katie set her eyes to maximum surprise and increased her blink-rate.

'Are they?'

'Yes. Is something going on between them?'

'They enjoy each other's company, if that's what you mean.'

110

Mr Lucas made an apologetic gesture.

'I'm sorry, Katie. I'm putting you in a difficult position, aren't I?'

'Are you, sir?'

'Yes, and I ought to know better. I'm pleased that Briony's found friends so quickly – and loyal friends at that.'

Katie blushed. Mr Lucas's compliment almost made her feel guilty about what she was up to – but not quite.

Phase One of Katie's plan was up and running; Phase Two got underway as soon as Mum came in from work. Katie had chosen her expression with great care, and as soon as Mum saw it, she said, 'Katie – what have you done now?'

'Nothing!'

'Come off it, I know that look. Are you in trouble at school?'

'Not exactly.'

Mum sat down next to Katie on the sofa, and went into all-understanding mode.

'Whatever it is, I'm sure it's not as bad as you think. Problems always appear bigger than they are when you keep them to yourself. Let's talk it through calmly, and—'

'It's Mr Lucas!' Katie blurted.

'Briony's father?'

'Yes.'

'Your English teacher?'

'That Mr Lucas, yes. He wants you to go and see him after school on Friday.'

'Why?'

'He's making appointments with all his pupils' parents,' Katie said, improvising. 'He's keen to meet them so he can show that even though he's new to the school, he can hack it.'

'I'm sure that he can,' said Mum. 'Tell him that I have every faith in his ability, and that an appointment won't be necessary in my case. He must have plenty to do, without—'

'I think it would be better if you told him yourself, Mum. You know how teachers get.'

'I do?'

'Sure you do! It's important for Mr Lucas to make a good impression, forge strong links with the community.'

'You're talking in clichés,' Mum said suspiciously. 'That's what people do when they're trying to pull the wool over someone's eyes!'

'I'm telling it like it is!' said Katie, then she brought out her Ultimate Weapon. 'Of course, if you're too busy, don't bother! If you can't organise your work so that you can spare a few minutes between half-three and four on Friday afternoon to discuss your daughter's future—'

'Spare me the blackmail, Katie! I surrender!'

Katie beamed.

'Good!'

Mum massaged her temples with the fingers of her left hand.

'You'll like him,' said Katie. 'He's nice.'

'Who is?'

'Mr Lucas.'

'All that concerns me is that he teaches you properly,' Mum said coldly. 'Liking and nice-ness are neither here nor there.'

'They don't hurt though, do they?'

'My top priority is my relationship with you, Katie. Mr Lucas only has to teach you, I have to live with you.'

Katie had forebodings. Mum seemed to have made up her mind that she and Mr Lucas weren't going to get along. If there was such a thing as instant attraction, did instant repulsion exist as well – and if it did, how could it work between two people who hadn't even met?

16

Over the next couple of days, time went weird on Katie. She'd noticed the phenomenon before: whenever she had something to look forward to, time dragged its feet and passed slowly; then, when what she'd been looking forward to finally arrived, time speeded up so that it was over in a flash.

The situation with Dave didn't help. Seeing him around school was slow torture. They smiled at each other and said hello, but there was no chance to be together and phone calls were no substitute for an in-person heart-to-heart. Katie began to feel insecure, and when she thought about her and Dave – which she did constantly – doubts came crawling out of the woodwork.

How was she going to measure up to Caitlin, the holiday wonder-girl who'd picked Dave up and turned his life around? Caitlin might not have broken Dave's heart but she'd certainly put a massive dent in it. Was he over her yet? Dave had mentioned that Caitlin and Katie looked alike – was that why he was interested? Was Katie a Caitlin-substitute, a next-best-thing? She knew she ought to ask Dave straight out, but what if it hadn't occurred to him?

Asking him might make him see that Katie was right, and then where would she be?

Thursday evening, as she was helping Mum cook dinner, Katie said, 'Mum, suppose someone liked you, but you thought that the only reason they liked you was because you reminded them of someone else they liked – would that be the same as if they *really* liked you?'

'Pass,' said Mum.

'How do people know when they like one another anyway?'

'I don't know, they just do. It's the same as making friends. Some people become close friends, others stay as acquaintances, sometimes the friendship develops into love. That's what happened to your father and me. Love comes in all shapes and sizes. You can't predict it because it affects different people in different ways.'

'*But who I am, Or who she is, Or why it happened, Only the gods can say,*' Katie murmured. 'So if you can't predict love, how d'you know when you're in it?'

'You get soppy,' Mum said. 'Even corny things like candlelit suppers for two seem like a good idea.'

'I guess romance must be pretty romantic.'

'You'll find out for yourself one day.'

Mum sniffed and reached up to wipe a tear from her cheek.

'Hey, don't cry, Mum!'

'I'm not crying, I'm slicing an onion,' Mum said.

Friday: the Big Day. Katie was hyper; her stomach was full of kittens and her mood swung between gloom and total despair.

'What if it goes wrong?' she asked Max and Briony at lunch-time.

'Then you'll have failed and the whole exercise will have been a waste of time,' Max said.

'Gee thanks, Max! I knew I could depend on you.'

Briony was more sympathetic.

'You've done all you can, Katie. The rest is up to them.'

'Lighten up a little!' said Max. 'Think about it objectively. What's the worst thing that can happen?'

'They both turn against me,' Katie said. 'I'll be completely humiliated and Mum will never talk to me again.'

'There!' said Max. 'Every cloud has a silver lining, if you look hard enough.'

As Katie was walking down from the Drama Suite at the end of the day, she met Dave walking up.

'Katie, you want to go to the cinema tomorrow, catch that movie we missed last week? Or would you rather do something else – like ice-skating? D'you skate?'

'No,' said Katie. 'Do you like me, Dave?'

Dave was taken aback.

'Like you?'

'Yeah, as in being round me is nicer than not.'

'Of course I like you, Katie. I've liked you since Year Seven.'

'Only I've been doing some thinking, and if you're just going out with me because you miss Caitlin, I have to tell you that— Year *Seven*?'

'On the first day, when we were all lined up in the tennis courts, waiting for our form tutors to collect us? I saw you talking to Max. He said something that made you laugh, you threw back your head and the sun shone through your hair, and I thought – I'm going to get to know that girl.'

'And it took you three years?'

'It was worth the wait.'

'Why d'you like me?'

'No idea, but I think finding out could be fun.'

'Is it because I look like Caitlin?'

'Other way round. I got involved with Caitlin because she looked like you. I wanted her to be another you, but you can't do that. You have to take people for who they are.'

'And who am I?'

'Once upon a time you were my Dream Girl, now you're Katie. I can talk to you the way I can't talk to anyone else. You understand stuff.'

A group of home-going Year Nine girls walked past. Two of them looked over their shoulders at Katie and Dave and broke into giggles.

'Talking of talking, we're talking,' Katie said.

'Is that what it's called?'

'I mean we're talking here, in school, where people can see us.'

'I don't have a problem with that.'

'But they'll think we're a couple.'

'I want them to think we're a couple. I want *us* to think we're a couple.'

'I'll have to think about that,' Katie said, frowning.

'Well, while you're doing it, think about this,' said Dave.

And he kissed her, right there in front of everybody, in full view of the coach queues, the staffroom and the gridlocked cars of the parents who'd come to pick up their children. It wasn't a full-blown kiss, just a quick brushing of lips, but it was a school First.

Katie was bewildered.

'Sorry!' said Dave. 'I got carried away for a second.'

'It's OK.'

'Are you offended?'

'No, but d'you know what I'll do if you ever try that again?'

'What?'

'I'll kiss you back,' said Katie. 'But can we please do it somewhere more private?'

★

Mum turned up at three-thirty precisely and found Katie waiting for her in the car park. Mum got out of the car and said, 'And you're here because?'

'I thought you might need help finding the English Suite.'

'I would if I didn't know where it is, but I do, so I don't. I can manage by myself. Why don't you go home?'

'I might as well stick around, cadge a lift.'

'No,' Mum said.

'But—'

'You won't stick around, you'll hover outside the door and try to listen in.'

'Would I do something like that?'

'Yes. Go home, Katie.'

Mum marched off towards Main Block.

'Mum!' said Katie. 'You're going the wrong way. The English Suite is over there!' She pointed.

'Thank you!' said Mum, changing direction without breaking step.

Katie took her time on the way home, thought about Dave and replayed the kiss over and over. She hadn't had him pegged as an impulsive kind of guy, but there were a lot of things she didn't know about Dave, and a few things that she hadn't known about herself. Contrary to her expectations, being kissed in front of the whole school hadn't been fatally embarrassing, and anyone who gave her stick because of it was going to limp away badly mauled.

Halfway through opening the front door, Katie heard the phone ring. She rushed to answer it, hoping for Dave and getting Liz Ricks.

Liz sounded peeved.

'So!' she said.

'So?'

'You and Dave Michaels.'

'Yeah.'

'You admit it then?'

'Why wouldn't I?'

'I can't keep up!' Liz grumbled. 'First it was Max and Briony, then it was Jasmine and Gavin, now it's you and Dave ... How's it done, Katie?'

'How is what done?'

'How d'you get off with a boy? I keep trying, but I can't seem to get the hang of it.'

'It's easy. Find a boy you fancy, wait outside his house, then when he comes out, act like you just happened to be strolling by ...'

'And?'

'Trip him over and jump on him,' Katie said.

Mum was home by four fifteen. She'd hardly crossed the threshold when Katie said, 'How did it go?'

'It went!' Mum grunted, wrinkling her nose.

'What did Mr Lucas say?'

'Plenty. He does go on, doesn't he? He says

120

you're coping well, apart from your tendency to take work too seriously.'

'My what?'

'He thinks you should be more laid-back, or you might suffer from student burn-out.'

'Excuse me?'

'You have to learn where to draw the line between conscientiousness and obsession.'

'Hang on, this was *me* you were talking about?'

'Mr Lucas did all the talking. I swear he's got verbal diarrhoea. If I was stuck in a class-room with him as my teacher, he'd drive me round the bend! Thank goodness I didn't let you talk me into inviting him over for a meal. That man could smarm at Olympic level.'

'So you didn't—? You and he weren't—?'

'Briony has my sympathy. She has to put up with him every day.'

'But don't you think he's a bit—?'

'I don't want to think about him at all. I've done more than my fair share of parental duties for the day. Care to join me vegging-out in front of the TV tonight? We'll call for a pizza delivery.'

'Er, I've got homework to do.'

'Leave it till Sunday. Chill, while you've got the chance,' said Mum. 'Who's this boy you were snogging after school?'

'Who told you?'

'Mr Bigmouth Lucas.'

'We weren't snogging!'

'Let's not get bogged down in technicalities – what's his name?'

Katie gritted her teeth; she was in for a long, gruelling evening.

17

The routine of the Saturday morning trek around the supermarket with Mum gave Katie a chance to be philosophical. Her plan had come to nothing, and hindsight told her that it had been a lousy plan in the first place. Matchmaking was impossible, because even though you might convince yourself that two people were perfect for each other, if they didn't have that vital spark between them, there was no match. Mum had been bang-on: liking, attraction, love, whatever, was unpredictable. Who would have figured that Briony could make Max forget about his crush on Jasmine, or that Jasmine and Gavin would get together, or that Katie would change her mind about Dave? Well, not change her mind, but see him clearly for the first time. You could never tell with love. It wasn't so much a flight to the stars on Cupid's wings as a blunder through thick fog at night, with sunglasses on.

'Going out tonight?' asked Mum, dropping a box of cat-crunchies into the trolley.

'Yeah. I'm meeting Dave at seven. What time's your do?'

'Eight. I'm being picked up at seven-thirty.'

'We'll probably go to the movies, unless— *Picked up?*'

'Mm.'

'You mean you're going *with* someone?'

'It's a dinner-dance,' Mum said. 'I couldn't go on my own, Mike Livingstone would ask me for a dance and be all over me.'

'Hold it right there!' Katie grabbed Mum by the shoulders and turned her so that they were face to face. 'Are you telling me you have a date tonight?'

'Mm.'

'With a man?'

'Yes, with a man.'

'But – who? When? Why? How?'

Mum wriggled free of Katie's grip and consulted the shopping list.

'I forgot fabric softener. Would you mind slipping back for a bottle please, Katie?'

'You're not changing the subject and I'm not slipping anywhere until you tell me more about this bloke you're going out with.'

Mum sighed.

'There's nothing to tell. He's a friend, he's at a loose end tonight, so I invited him to the dinner-dance. Office do's are always the same – people only talk about work. If I'm with Simon, the conversation will be more varied.'

'His name's Simon?'

'Yes.'

'Is he one of the guys from work?'

'No.'

'Where did you meet him?'

'Does it matter? We met, OK? Stop badgering me!'

'When do I get to meet him?'

'You don't.'

'Why not?'

'Because he's *my* friend and it's *my* business, so butt out!'

'Have you been out with him before?'

'Fabric softener.'

'How long has this been going on? Is it serious?'

'Fabric softener,' Mum repeated. 'Dinner-dances are here and gone in an instant, but washing needs doing forever.'

'Oh, I get it! It's cool for you to cross-examine me about Dave, but I'm not allowed to ask you about this Simon bloke.'

'You can ask me all you like. I don't have to answer.'

'That's not fair!'

'I'm your mother, I'm allowed to be unfair,' Mum said.

While Mum was busy restocking the cupboards, Katie borrowed the mobile from Mum's handbag and went up to her bedroom to phone Max.

'Max? Katie. Zip on Mum and Mr L, but—'

'Hello?' said Max. 'Will whoever's calling please adjust their communication device for Planet Earth?'

'Mum can't stand Mr Lucas. She's going out tonight with someone called Simon.'

'Good for her!'

'Not good, Max. According to Mum they're just friends, but then she would say that, wouldn't she? I don't know anything about the guy. What if he's a geek? What if he wears nerdy little glasses, and socks and sandals? *What if he's got a beard?'*

'Inhale deeply and remain calm,' Max said in his guru-voice. 'Embrace your fear until it becomes your friend.'

'How can I be calm? This is an emergency – help!'

'You're jumping to conclusions. Maybe they are friends, like your mum said. Maybe he's all right. Does your mum go for dogs?'

'Not usually.'

'He's probably good-looking then.'

'But he might not be! Mum's always saying that personality matters more than looks.'

'She lied, they both matter. You need to check this guy out.'

'I know, but how? He's picking Mum up half an hour after I'm supposed to meet Dave.'

'OK, ring Dave, tell him you're going to be late and be in the house when Simon arrives.'

'Oh yeah, like Mum's going to let me do that! She won't even answer any questions about him.'

'On the defensive, huh? They're more than friends.'

126

'That's what I figured.'

'OK, ring Dave, say you'll be late, leave the house at the time you were going to leave, hide somewhere and watch.'

'Are you suggesting that I spy on my own mother?'

'Yeah.'

'She'll freak!'

'Only if she finds out,' Max said.

Katie ended the call and started to ring Dave.

'What do you want for lunch?' Mum shouted up the stairs.

'I'll make myself a sandwich. Down in a minute!'

No one was in at the Michaels' residence. Katie waited for the answering-machine to finish its message and after the beep sounded she said, 'This is Katie with a message for Dave. I won't be able to make it until eight o'clock tonight. Something's come up. Family thing. I'll tell you about it when I see you. Bye!'

Kate's conscience pricked her. Why was she so worked-up? She'd been nagging Mum to find someone for months, and now that she had, Katie was panicking. She ought to be happy for Mum, and she had absolutely no right to sneak around, prying into her mother's private affairs.

But she was going to – no question.

At half-six, Katie knocked on the bathroom door.

'Mum? I'm off.'

'Have a good time!' Mum said above the hissing of the shower.

'You too. See you!'

Katie left the house, took two paces down the street and came to a halt. Somewhere between the excitement and guilt she felt over what she was about to do to Mum, she'd neglected an important detail – she had an hour to kill and no idea of how to kill it. She should have brought her personal stereo with her, but if she went back for it, Mum's suspicions might be aroused.

Katie walked on, trying to look as though she were on her way somewhere. As she walked, she considered her choice of hiding-place. The phone box on the corner was a possibility; she could pretend to be ringing someone; but the phone box was a hundred metres from the house. Katie would have to turn her head to keep watch, and since the box was lit there was a risk that Mum might spot her.

The best place would be the Tremletts' front garden. It was directly opposite Katie's house, and had a privet hedge she could crouch behind. Katie knew the Tremletts quite well because she cat-sat for them when they went on holiday. They were a sweet elderly couple; she was sure they wouldn't mind her occupying the garden for a few minutes.

Katie wandered through the estate. Saturday

evening was well underway: TV lights shining through front windows; people walking their dogs; kids playing football on a patch of grass.

Katie bought a can of Diet Coke at the newsagents in the precinct, parked herself on a convenient wall and drank the Coke in tiny sips to make it last. At ten-past seven she dropped the empty can in a litter-bin and headed back home. Her timing was immaculate, she was in position behind the Tremletts' hedge by seven-twenty.

At seven twenty-seven a car cruised along the street and slowed as it approached Katie's house. She held her breath – family saloon, nothing flash; the orange of the streetlights made it difficult for her to make out the colour. The driver's face was in shadow, so—

'Katie?'

Katie's head whipped around. Her heart thumped like the hooves of a thoroughbred racehorse on the final straight.

Mr Tremlett was standing on his doorstep, looking puzzled.

'Er, hello, Mr Tremlett!' Katie said in a hoarse whisper.

'What are you doing?'

'I, ah, um, I'm . . . looking for an earring! I was brushing my hair, and the brush caught my ear, and my earring sort of pinged over your hedge.'

'Earring?' said Mr Tremlett, looking even more puzzled. 'I didn't know you wore earrings. I was saying to Mrs Tremlett the other day that you're not like those young girls who go around with bits of metal stuck in them.'

'No, I don't normally wear earrings, do I? These are clip-ons. I borrowed them from my mum.'

'Shall I help you look?'

'No, no, I'll be fine!'

'Sounds like you've got a sore throat. Are you coming down with a cold?'

'Singing in the bath!' Katie said. 'Must have overdone it. Oh, here's the earring, look!' She mimed fitting something to her right ear. 'Phew! Just as well I found it. Mum wouldn't be pleased if it got lost.'

'I don't expect she would.'

'Well, I'd better be on my way.'

'Right you are.'

'Must get a move on, or I'll be late.'

'You wouldn't want to be late.'

'No. So, er, I'll be going then.'

Katie couldn't put it off any longer. She straightened up, and her eyes cleared the top of the hedge at the exact moment that the car turned out of sight at the end of the street.

Katie told Dave the whole story at Manconi's. It lasted for two cups of cappuccino.

When it was over, Dave said, 'You staked-out your own house? That's a bit drastic, isn't it?'

'I felt like I was casing the joint!' said Katie.

'And it was pointless. I was interrupted, so I didn't see the guy.'

'Are you always that underhand?'

'Pretty much – except with you. Mostly when it comes to my mum.'

'It must run in the family.'

'Meaning?'

'Your mum's been pretty underhand about her new boyfriend. I'd say you were both quits.'

'Hey, when you put it like that, I guess you're right. Mum had it coming. Never again though! Too nerve-wracking.'

'It needn't be,' said Dave. 'You could always wait up until your mum gets dropped off, and catch them then.'

Katie's jaw dropped.

'Why didn't I think of that?'

'Stick with me, kid!' said Dave. 'I'll make you a star.'

As it turned out, Dave didn't make Katie a star, but he did make her feel special by doing ordinary things – hanging out and talking – and some extraordinary things, such as progressing to Level Two kissing on a bench near the river.

'I never thought this would happen,' said Dave. 'I used to have dreams about kissing you.'

'Is it better or worse than you expected?'

'I wasn't expecting anything, so it's unexpected.'

Katie looked up at the sky.

'There's a new moon.'

'Oh yeah! You're meant to turn over the money in your pockets when you see a new moon.'

'Why?'

'Beats me. It's something my grandad told me.'

'I thought you were supposed to wish on the new moon.'

'So make a wish!'

Katie started to, then laughed.

'D'you realise we've been kissing under the new moon, Dave? How corny is that?'

But it wasn't corny, it was romantic.

When Katie got home, she turned on the TV and dozed off on the sofa. The sound of a car pulling up outside woke her. She glanced at her watch – 23:55 – and went out into the hall. Footsteps, voices and laughter advanced up the front path and stopped in the porch. Through the frosted glass panel of the door, Katie saw two silhouettes meet in an embrace. She stepped forwards, worked the lock and opened the front door.

There was Mum, blinking in the light, looking just this side of tipsy and as startled as a teenager caught making-out.

The man in her arms was—

'*Mr Lucas?*' Katie squeaked.

'E-e-r, hello Katie,' said Mr Lucas. 'Have you had a nice evening?'

132

18

Mr Lucas bottled out, made a hasty exit and left Mum to face Katie. Mum clocked the look in Katie's eyes, winced and turned the wince into a sway.

'I may have had a glass of wine too many,' she said, attempting a slur. 'I should go to bed and sleep it off.'

'I'll make you a cup of coffee. We need to talk.'

'I'm not really up to it. Can't it wait until—?'

'You're overdoing the drunk-act,' said Katie. 'Into the lounge and sit down, now! You owe me an explanation, young lady.'

Katie was still fuming when she handed Mum a mug of strong black coffee, but let her take two swigs before she started in.

'What's the story, Mum? Are you and Mr Lucas—?'

'Seeing each other? Yes.'

'So are you friends or what?'

'I'm not sure what we are yet.'

'Then what was all that stuff yesterday? You made like you hated his guts.'

'That was a wind-up. Simon and I thought you deserved it.'

'Why?'

'For being so manipulative and sticking your beak in where it wasn't wanted.'

'I can't believe you did that! I was trying to do you a favour, and you were laughing at me behind my back. What kind of trick is that?'

'A mean and deceitful trick,' Mum admitted. 'Amusing though. You've made me squirm often enough with your schemes to pair me off. It was refreshing to turn the tables.'

'You made me feel like a total dipstick!'

'Will an apology suffice, or would you like me to turn myself in at the police station?'

Katie grunted. Annoyed as she was at being outmanoeuvred by Mum, there was still a lot she wanted to know, so she lowered her grumpiness a notch and said, 'How did you and Mr Lucas first meet?'

'It was your fault. I was furious with you when you tried to set me up with that bouncer, but afterwards I began to think that you might have a point. In three years I'll be forty-one, you'll probably be away at university, and what will I have in my life? A job and an empty house to come home to.'

'There's Cleo,' Katie said.

'Please, no jokes! I'm pouring my heart out here. Anyway, to avoid your causing me any more humiliation, I decided to have a shot at finding a partner for myself.'

'You put an ad in a Lonely Hearts column?' said Katie. 'What did it say?'

'I didn't put an ad anywhere,' Mum said. 'I contacted a computer dating agency—'

Katie had a memory-flash: the non-bill bill that Mum had been so reluctant to open.

'—and they put me in touch with Simon. He wrote to the agency the same day that I did, because he was fed up with Briony nagging him to get a life. The agency matched us up, we had our first date last Saturday, we clicked and the rest you know.'

'Why didn't you tell me?'

'For the same reason you didn't tell me about Dave. I didn't want you to make a fuss before there was anything to make a fuss about.'

'Nah! My mum is dating my English teacher – why would I stress over that? Have you snogged him?'

'That's off-limits.'

'Watch your step. Some men are only interested in one thing.'

'Don't tease me, Katie! This is hard enough as it is.'

Mum glanced at the photo of Dad, the glance became a stare and she drifted away somewhere; Katie knew where.

'He wouldn't mind,' she said quietly.

'Who?'

'Dad – about you and Mr Lucas. He'd be pleased.'

'Think so?'

'I know so.' Katie mentally crossed her

fingers as she prepared to say what she should have said long before. 'Mum, it's time you took those pictures down. You don't need photographs to remember Dad, and neither do I.'

'I know.'

'And you don't need to keep his clothes in the wardrobe. They're not him. Stick them in the loft or take them to a charity shop.'

'You're right, but—'

'There are no buts, Mum. You have to let him go.'

Mum looked forlorn.

'I know I do, and I'm trying, but it isn't easy to start again at my age. Meeting someone new, dating, worrying about being stood up – I'd forgotten all that.'

'I'm always here to give you advice.'

Mum laughed.

'Care to give me some right now?'

'Sure! When in doubt, kiss under a new moon.'

'Does it work?'

'It did for me,' Katie said.

Katie devoted Sunday morning to getting her homework done, then after lunch she met up with Max. They went for a walk around the lake at the back of the estate, and Katie gave Max an update.

'Your mum put one over on you?' Max said. 'I love it!'

'Yeah, yeah! Gloat, why don't you?'

'What's the matter – lost your SOH?'

'Only temporarily. I know that one day I'll look back on this and my toes will curl.'

Max bent down to pick up a pebble, and skimmed it over the surface of the water.

'Hey, Katie, what if they get married? That would make Briony your stepsister, wouldn't it? Weird!'

'Not so fast, Max! They've only been out together twice. I don't think they're planning the honeymoon just yet.'

'They might get married though.'

'I'll deal with that if and when I come to it.'

'How long before it's all round school?'

'Not long – especially if I make an announcement in Year Ten assembly.'

'Don't be so melodramatic! All it'll take is a word to Liz Ricks. Crazy, isn't it?'

'Absolutely. What's crazy?'

'At the end of the summer we were looking for a guy with a GSOH who WLTM someone like your mum, when *we* didn't have a love-life. Now I'm fixed-up with Briony, you're fixed-up with Dave and your mum fixed herself up.'

'I was wrong about the GSOH thing,' Katie admitted. 'It's part of it, but it's not the whole deal. You have to have trust, and understanding, and mutual respect, and . . .' Her voice trailed off.

'You're thinking,' said Max.

'I'm always thinking.'

'No, you're *thinking* thinking. Spill!'

'I was wondering about something Liz said to me. D'you reckon that she gossips about other people's relationships because she hasn't got one of her own?'

'Could be – why?'

'Because if she did have a relationship of her own, there might be less goss. Maybe we should help her get together with someone. Like Greg Ross – have you noticed what happens to his eyes when he looks at her?'

Max laughed.

'You're doing it again, Katie! You never give up, do you?'

'No,' said Katie. 'Not ever.'